PRAISE FOR JOSIP NOVAKOVICH

"Novakovich knows how to tell a story, and his prose has an easy, elegant velocity."

—*The New York Times*

"Like Aleksandar Hemon and Ha Jin, short story writer Novakovich manages the feat of writing vibrantly and inventively in a second language, shaping English to the dictates of his satiric, folk-tinged storytelling."

—*Publishers Weekly*

"One of the most forceful and original essayists in the English language."

—*Los Angeles Review of Books*

"Novakovich's characters…are generous, flawed, violent, and rooted in an understanding of the earth."

—*Montreal Review of Books*

"There are very few native-born English speakers who write as well."

—*The Guardian*

HERITAGE
OF SMOKE

ALSO BY JOSIP NOVAKOVICH

HERITAGE OF SMOKE

JOSIP NOVAKOVICH

DZANC
BOOKS

5220 Dexter Ann Arbor Rd.
Ann Arbor, MI 48103
www.dzancbooks.org

First US edition: January 2017

Library of Congress Cataloging-in-Publication Data

Names: Novakovich, Josip, 1956- author.
Title: Heritage of smoke / Josip Novakovich.
Other titles: Ex-YU
Description: Ann Arbor, MI : Dzanc Books, 2017.
Identifiers: LCCN 2016027570 | ISBN 9781941088661 (softcover)
Subjects: | BISAC: FICTION / Short Stories (single author). | FICTION /
    Literary. | FICTION / War & Military. | FICTION / Cultural Heritage.
Classification: LCC PS3564.O914 E9 2017 | DDC 813/.54--dc23
LC record available at https://lccn.loc.gov/2016027570

Printed in the United States of America

10   9   8   7   6   5   4   3   2   1

To Eva and Joseph

TABLE OF CONTENTS

WHITE MOUSTACHE

The Second World War ended eleven years before my birth, and by the time I could follow conversations, people still talked as though the war hadn't ended. Silver-haired men limped in the streets like incompetent ghosts who'd lost the ability to float. Even then, I didn't believe in ghosts, but that was the metaphor that worked for me as I looked at these broken men. Some of them used walking sticks, and all of them smoked, and as they contemplated the hardship of their retirement, smoke came out of their nostrils, mouths, ears, and hairs.

Behind curtained windows, old women clad in black looked out into the streets, and the flimsy curtains created an illusion of smoke rising from the ground in which the remains of the war were buried. The remains weren't buried well, and they emitted so much smoke and whiteness. Most houses were coated in white stucco, but they invariably changed to sooty gray and black and collected fine black particles on their windows. It was hard to breathe from all the soot and smoke and steam, and the men who walked in the streets cleared their throats and spat out green phlegm as though bits of clay had remained in them after their incomplete resurrections.

One of these ethereal silver-haired men was Branko, my aunt's husband. He'd moved to Zagreb and built his house of red brick. He locked his rusty iron door with several large clangy keys. At the age of fifteen I visited him, despite knowing that he was a relentless talker. He enquired about my grades and plans for the future, and was dismayed that I planned to become an architect.

"What can you build in socialism that's not ugly?" he asked.

"Ugly can be beautiful if you look at it long enough," I replied.

"Why would you say something like that?"

He left his mouth open, and I admired the fact that he had all his teeth, that his hair was thick, combed back in tidy waves. His head was disproportionately big and, like most people with big jaws, he had a loud voice. Maybe he was loud because he was half deaf from explosions in the war.

As we were finishing a green bean soup, he said, "There are spirits all around us."

"I don't believe in ghosts."

"You haven't lived enough to know."

"I'm surprised that you, as a religious person, could believe fairy tales."

"If I didn't believe in ghosts, how could I be religious? Religion is a host for ghosts, but there are wild ghosts, like the ones you can invoke in a séance. We had a neighbour like that when we started out. If you visited him, he'd try to terrify you by calling in the ghosts—well, one particular ghost."

"Oh, Branko, please don't go into that again," said my aunt.

She and Branko never had children, and that made him (rather than her) hysterical. She quietly observed with a slight smile, her seemingly black eyes sparkling. Her braids were as thick as the ropes used for docking ships in the Rijeka harbor.

"You stay out of it," he said. "He needs to know. Communists aren't telling the truth to these children."

She sat at a table in the next room, with the doors open so she could listen, and measured material for clothes, drawing a pattern with white chalk to dress an absent body.

"Marxists are materialists, they don't believe in spirits," I said.

"And you want to be like them?" Branko said. "Let me tell you, they've turned people into ghosts, and for them to teach you that there are no ghosts and spirits is another atrocity."

He drank Turkish coffee with muddy grains at the bottom of the cup. When his silver moustache emerged, it looked like a brush that had just been dipped into brown paint. He would now paint in broad strokes, from his hidden upper lip.

After the war, Branko began, we couldn't afford to have a home all to ourselves so we rented a room from Borovnik, a carpenter, between the synagogue and the Lutheran Evangelical church. The church was empty and its windows were smashed, and shards were scattered inside and outside of it. At the end of the war most local Germans were deported, and the few who remained didn't want to be identified as Germans and nobody took care of the church. The synagogue was no longer a temple but a bowling alley for the foundry workers, and all day long you heard balls hitting pins and workers swearing sacrilegiously. One evening, just after I paid rent, I was sitting in my landlord's kitchen drinking coffee when suddenly there was banging on the door—not soft banging, such as a fist coated in flesh would make, but sharp, like a stick or a bare bone hitting the wood.

Borovnik smiled and said, "Won't you open it for me? I'm old and it's hard for me to get up out of my chair."

It was quiet now. Only his wheezing could be heard. He leaned, sitting on the edge of his ornately carved armchair, which had snakeheads for armrests. I stood up and opened the door, but there was nobody there. Right in front of his doorstep, the cobbles stopped and dirt road began. There were no lights in the synagogue, and the large windows of the Lutheran church loomed empty. The chilly outdoors smelled like a dialogue of tomcats.

"There's nobody, just a cat," I told Borovnik.

"He comes here every night and knocks like that," he said.

"The cat? He'd have to be the size of a lion."

"No. The ghost. He doesn't want to leave me in peace."

"How would you know it's a ghost?" I asked Borovnik and closed the door. "Do you want me to lock it?"

"You don't have to. He wouldn't want to come in. He hated it here when he used to live up in the attic."

"In the attic? Don't give me such clichés, please!"

I sat down and didn't know what to say, and Borovnik stared at me with his reddish eyes. He wasn't albino, but you wouldn't know that by looking at him—his skin had become pale and the edges of his eyelids were translucent. His eyes were bloodshot from sawdust, and there was sawdust in the hairs of his hawkish nose.

Suddenly there was another loud and sharp knock on top of the doorframe.

I jumped to my feet and opened the door and there was nobody there, but the smell of the tomcat was even greater. I pulled the door gently but it slammed against the frame so that the house shook. The white mortar around the doorframe cracked further and some sand shuddered loose, trickling to the floor.

My host rubbed his purplish hands. "Ha, what do you say now?"

"I think there was a gust of wind, a change of seasons."

"Oh, no. The knock comes from far above the door—it's a ghost, passing above the ground, like an angel of death in Egypt marking every house where a first-born should be slain."

Out of curiosity, I opened the door again and, out there, the wind was picking up and a dust storm was developing. From the dirt road, dust blew onto the cobbles and the evergreens in the hills whistled in distress.

"See, it's the wind," I said. "Some branch got rattled."

"There's no tree next to my house. There used to be trees but we cut them down in the war, in 1942, to stay warm. When you don't have enough to eat in the cold, you need even more firewood."

Soon I learned who Borovnik's ghost was. It was an angel of death marking a house in Egypt; he was right about that. A man's death needed to be paid for with another death. Maybe Borovnik thought he was speaking allegorically, but there was no difference between the allegory and the events. Have you seen how large the Jewish cemetery on the outskirts of Daruvar is? If you look at the dates, most people there died in 1941 and 1942. Well, Borovnik was hiding a Jewish watchmaker by the name of Bergman.

Borovnik cut a deal with the watchmaker; he would save him, in exchange for some woodworking labor and half of his watches once the war was over. During the day, he had Bergman work in the basement, making fine engravings in tables and armchairs. If Bergman complained, Borovnik threatened to turn him in to the Germans.

One evening, the Ustasha army went through town with the Germans, and as a courtesy the Ustashas gave all their garrison space to the Germans and slept instead in the school, save for some who slept in private homes of people they knew. So several soldiers who trusted Borovnik as a peaceful carpenter came over to his house to spend the night. As they sat around the table and drank slivovitz, about a dozen clocks struck midnight in the attic, and they kept banging.

"How many clocks do you have?" asked one soldier, and another, "Why are you hiding them in the attic? If we go up there and find that you're hiding Jews, we'll shoot you. We'll find out anyway, so you better not lie. If you tell us the truth, we won't shoot you."

Borovnik said, "I have a tenant up there just for a couple of days. I let him come up to fix a clock. Leave him alone and you can have all my slivovitz."

The Ustashas went up to the attic and dragged down Bergman, who blinked in the light. He was old but his beard was still black. They took him out, and maybe they took him to the train station and shipped him to Auschwitz or maybe they shot him in the woods. Anyhow, I couldn't find his name in the Jewish cemetery later on. Borovnik's story bothered me, so I wanted to find out where Bergman ended up. But I couldn't find his name anywhere. It was as though he'd never existed.

"The Ustashas took away all the clocks but this one," Branko concluded. "This one. Borovnik gave it to me because he couldn't bear listening to it strike. I couldn't either, so I took out the banging mechanism. I let it run out of its tension and didn't rewind it. I don't like to listen to it tick. Even that is too loud, each tick like a bang, and that drives me crazy."

"Why do you keep it then?" I asked.

"It looks beautiful. Just look at it."

It was true—the woodwork was amazingly convoluted, and if you stared enough into it, you'd see cat paws, with claws sticking out, and an owl head, and acorns.

"You just don't throw something like that away," Branko said. "And the time, well the time stopped for us then, in that war. We pretend it's gone on, but it hasn't. It shouldn't go on. And God hasn't let it go on. The time is out."

"Come on. You're overdoing it, don't you think?"

"Oh, you're young and naïve. All your hair is black, how can you talk? Wait for your own horrors—and they will come, they will come—before you talk. Anyway," Branko went on, "Borovnik had no peace for years after the war. Even his eyebrows and moustache turned white. Bergman knocked on his door every evening. A month after my first visit to him, Borovnik died. During the funeral, the otherwise indifferent and quiet white horses the town used for funerals went wild and dragged the hearse in a gallop. The wheels went off and the hearse turned over. Pallbearers carried the casket to the grave. They said it was incredibly light, that most likely Borovnik's body wasn't in the casket. I think it evaporated into a ghost. The animals felt that; they are attuned to the otherworldly better than most of us."

"Were you scared that Borovnik would haunt you?" I asked Branko.

"I thought he would, but then, he was so ghostlike in his life, he probably didn't want to duplicate it. Well, maybe the clock keeps him away."

"But your hair has turned white anyway. Why do you think hair turns white? Is it from worry? Lack of iron in the diet? Lack of wine?"

"No. Worry doesn't do anything. It's from horror, pure horror. You wonder why my hair is all white, like Borovnik's?"

"You actually believe that Borovnik saw a ghost?"

"I heard the ghost myself. Whenever I visited the carpenter, I heard the ghost. Borovnik joked that the ghost was fond of me, didn't want to miss me."

Branko raised his eyebrows, in amazement that someone could be doubting his experience. His eyebrows looked like crow wings over two setting suns; his light hazel eyes looked like setting suns filtered through the vapors of the day, which rose high to form white clouds out of his hair, which, despite all the glow, didn't reflect the color of the sun. While being a passive listener, I had all these images. Though he out-talked me and made it hard for me to participate in the conversation, he still couldn't take away my looking and imagining.

"There are many reasons why my hair turned white," Branko continued. "There are a hundred things, each of which could leave me tossing in my bed for the rest of the nights God gave me. But I'll tell you just two. Two brothers. And I won't mention fathers and mothers."

In the meanwhile, my aunt had finished making patterns in the cloth and she came in to wash her chalky hands in the sink. She walked into the garden, and she came back with white and yellow roses, which she put in a blue vase, gingerly, so they wouldn't prick her. Branko leaned over, burying his nose in the petals, and drew a deep breath, closing his eyes to better concentrate on the fragrance.

My youngest brother was drafted by the Ustashas. My family wasn't militaristic, and at that time you couldn't be a pacifist or a conscientious objector, and you'd end up in whatever army came to town first. All these armies went door to door, dragging young men out, stealing whatever there was to be stolen, and anyhow, that is how my brothers ended up in two different armies. The soldiers walked into the house, saw my younger brother kneading dough for bread, and forced him to be a cook. My other brother, Nikola, hid in the shed and was later drafted by the partisans. Until late 1943, the youngest one kept boiling potatoes, while the men who came from the forests boasted of their courage and taunted him as their *krumpiras*. The potato man. The tide of the war was turning with the Germans not being able to afford troops in Yugoslavia, and they no longer helped the Ustashas keep their positions against the partisans and the Chetniks. Some of the best-trained Ustasha forces had been spent in the battle of Stalingrad. So my brother the cook volunteered to become an infantryman. He was shot in his first day of action, a bullet through his lower abdomen. It didn't catch the spine or the kidneys. He was taken to the temporary hospital ward, in Daruvar, a blue building near the Catholic church. He was getting better, and his fever had subsided. The nurse gave him aspirin. He kept being thirsty and the nurse gave him seltzer water, which, together with the aspirin, ate through his wound.

I came in and asked, "Where is my brother?"

"He's dead," the nurse said.

"Impossible. He wasn't wounded badly and he was recovering."

"That's all true, but he died. He drank seltzer water, his wound opened up, and he bled to death. We could do nothing about it."

"All because of seltzer water? Couldn't you give him something else?"

"He asked for it, and we didn't know. Now we know. We won't repeat the mistake."

"How will that help him?"

It was clear by then which side was winning, and she probably contributed in her way, killing the wounded of the losing enemy. I couldn't afford to pay for a gravedigger, and the old town gravedigger was away, digging who knows where, so I made the coffin from an old cupboard, cutting it in half. I dug on the hill, on the edge of the cemetery, into the clay. You know how fine the clay is around Daruvar—you can make the best bricks out of it. There was no funeral. Almost everybody who could walk was in some kind of army, and the townspeople were nearly all incapable of walking, or they hid in terror. The outskirts of the town smoked from mortar fire. At night, partisans shelled the town from the mountain. I dragged the coffin on a little cart myself, like a horse. I placed him in the ground and covered him. I was too tired to make him a cross.

Branko stood up to make another cup of coffee. He beat the coffee beans into Turkish dust in an iron cup with a round-headed piece of iron, which looked like a bone, the head of a child's femur. The metal rang dull under the crunch of beans. Branko sprinkled the coffee powder into boiling water as though scattering ashes and the intoxicating smell of black dust wafted through the room. I declined a cup he offered because, from my experience, coffee smelled good but tasted horrid.

"Branko, what's come over you? He's too young to like coffee."

My aunt brought me a cup of milk with a slice of bread and a spoonful of honey. I let the honey trickle onto the buttered slice in concentric circles.

"He's too young to like anything," Branko said, before continuing his story.

What happened with my other brother, Nikola, was even worse. When he arrived at the partisan camp, he got old shoes that were too big for him. As he walked through the cold November mud, his feet froze. He asked for another pair of shoes.

"You have a fine pair of shoes," said his sergeant.

"They're too big."

"Wrap up an old towel around your feet, and they'll be warm."

"I tried, that didn't work. Could I go home and get my own pair?"

"You could have thought of that when you were drafted."

"I wasn't allowed to think. I had to go right away."

"What did you expect, that we would supply everything for you? That this is a paid-for picnic? You got to contribute."

"I'm eager to contribute, Kapetane."

"I'm not a captain but a sergeant. We can't afford to let you go. We need you in action here."

"But there's been no action, just walking."

"You don't need to explain to me what action is."

At night, Nikola walked out of the camp. He got exhausted a village before home, and as he knew an old man there, he knocked on his door late in the afternoon the following day.

The man opened the door, and said, "I thought you were in the partisans."

"I am, but I have to get my shoes."

"Have a seat, and I will make you a kajgana, with the best corn eggs and sour cream. First I need to go out to the stall to get the eggs, fresh out of the hen."

"You didn't pick them up in the morning?"

"You wouldn't believe my hens. They lay them even in the evening."

The man didn't come back for a long time and so Nikola went out, looking for him. Several partisans were in the yard, and one of them was beheading a chicken on a stump with a short-handled axe. The soldiers took bets as to whether the headless chicken would run and how far. It didn't run. That infuriated most of them.

"Pero, what do you feed your chickens? They should have more energy than this. How can you eat this? I bet the meat is all flabby."

My brother was about to slip out of the yard when the chicken beheader said, "Where the hell do you think you are going? You stay here. We were worried about you and we came here looking for you."

"Why did you leave?" another one asked Nikola.

"I didn't leave. I'm going home to get boots."

"What's wrong with the ones you have? They look fine."

"The sole is coming off." Nik lifted the boot and pulled the sole off in the front, and through it, his naked big toe peeked out. Small bent nails stuck out of the sole from all the sides, so it looked like the jaws of a sharp-toothed pike in the river about to swallow a chubby pink fish.

"You just pulled the sole off yourself. You can nail it all back together, it's simple."

"The boot is rotten, just look at the leather."

"Seems fine to me."

"I have a good solid pair of boots that will last me through the winter, so I was on the way home to get them."

"You could have told us you were going."

"I tried, but the sergeant wouldn't let me go."

"He couldn't—it's not in his authority. Anyway, you shouldn't waste anybody's time like that, with your tales. You were deserting, that's the simple fact."

"I'd come back tomorrow morning."

"Once you're home, you'll like it better there, or you might join another army."

Then they shot him, with one bullet to the head.

Branko paused, his eyes glazed with tears, and he stood up from the table and walked unsteadily to the bathroom, touching the walls for support. As he wore shorts, I saw that his legs were thin; he seemed to have no calves. Yet these thin legs had to support his big torso and huge head. He blew his nose and cleared his throat. He probably spat out green phlegm. I heard him brushing his teeth. His mouth must have grown weary and sticky from so much talking, so he refreshed it. My aunt offered me a walnut cake. She tried to smile but she was sniffling too.

"His memory is too good, and he remembers all the worst things, all the details," she said.

"But he wasn't there. He must be making it up," I said.

"Oh no, he heard lots of things and he saw too much. He was everywhere, trust me."

Branko limped back through the door, smelling of mint.

"That's a great cake," I said to my aunt, and hoped that Branko could be distracted from his histories. He put white cotton fluff into his ears as though he wouldn't need to listen to anything—for talking he didn't need to listen.

All these drafts give me earaches, he said. Anyway, now that I started to tell you what a doomed land this land of ours is, I must finish. So, they shot my brother with one bullet. They were saving bullets; that's all they gave him, one bullet, and so he died slowly while the soldiers took bets whether a man with a shot brain would crawl and how far he would manage to go before quitting. They were disappointed that he crawled only one yard, and they kicked him with their boots. He was buried in a field, in the soft clay, near the stream.

For ten years, we knew nothing about what happened to him. All we knew was that he'd been a partisan and that he'd vanished. We even boasted that he died as a freedom fighter for the new country. But there was no new country. Things here always remain the same.

After the war, I inquired about where Nik disappeared but was told repeatedly that there were too many missing people, that there was no way to recover all the bodies from the war.

One day in a tavern, however, a toothless man told me, lisping, "For a shot of slivovitz, I will let you know where your brother is buried." I bought him a bottle, and the man with sunken lips gave me his account of Nikola's execution.

"I was there," he said, "but could do nothing about it. I was sorry for your brother, but war is like that, full of sorrow you can do nothing about but drink for the rest of your life. Even then we were all drunk, and to tell you the truth, we were only pretending to be looking for your brother. We were sent there to find him but all we wanted to find was slivovitz, and if he hadn't come out, probably we would have gone back with the few bottles the old peasant gave us. The slivovitz made every bone crazy."

He pronounced his words badly, so *everyone* sounded like *every bone* and all the people, *svi ljudi*, like *svi ludi*. All humans, all hummus. Some of it may have been intentional. It was hard to follow his slurred speech, but I managed to reconstruct the story from it. I didn't believe the drunk. People often said *in vino veritas,* but I find *in vino exaggeration* to be true more often. I believe in coffee.

The drunk led me out into the field in Badljevina, near the train station and a lively stream. Weeping willows and pussy willows lined the stream and, in the setting sun, their yellow barks blazed like a golden fire, without a trace of red. The water gurgled like someone was clearing his throat, and I thought I saw silvery bodies of trout glistening as they leaped over rocks, but it was probably an illusion, with the waves occasionally flashing the light of the sun back at me from under the dark canopy of willows. Maybe I saw no real trout, but glimpses of trout spirits.

"We buried him here, by this willow," said the drunk.

"How do you know it's here?"

"I know it was near that tilting old willow, that's all."

And so I set out with a shovel to unearth my brother's bones. I was glad it had been several years since his death because bones I could deal with. Rotten flesh I couldn't.

I dug in some five feet and found nothing.

"You lied," I told the man.

"I didn't. Dig again. Maybe you're too far from the river." He was sitting on the tree roots and licking the bottleneck.

That time I didn't find anything, and I went back alone the following morning. First I fished and caught a trout. I released the trout back in the water so I could have my wish. I know that sounds superstitious, it's not a golden fish, but the trout was a rainbow trout, with beautiful sparkling colors, blues and purples.

After that, I dug again. The soil went smoothly from shovelful to shovelful. I cut through earthworms, struggled with a few tree roots, and I hit a bone. I dug out three skeletons. Was one of them my brother? I wondered. In our parts, nobody has good teeth, unlike the people from the coast, who get more sun and eat small fish bones. Here, with all the rains, everything rots, including our teeth. My brother, however, had a perfect set of teeth, large, white, in a good jaw. So when I saw a skull with all the teeth in it, not even now in any way marred, I knew it must be my brother.

I gathered his bones. I didn't have a car, so I packed them in a suitcase, and I carried them to the train station and waited for the steam-engine train. The train was late, but it didn't matter. I was struck with grief. That evening, the whole train was empty, but it stopped, and I dragged the bones. Well, not to make a short story long, let me tell you. I buried the bones right next to his brother's, with my own hands. We could have afforded a gravedigger—now there were many of them in town because after the war people kept dying very quickly, of all sorts of disease but mostly grief.

Before then, my hair was white, but my moustache was black. But after I buried my brother, even my moustache turned white.

Several years after Branko told me the causes of his grief, he died of a massive stroke; his brain burned out. And when I visited my aunt, she looked startled. Her large black eyes flashed, reflecting the sunlight of the day.

"You know," she said, "you look just like your father did, so at first I thought it was his ghost walking through the door. But then I decided there was too much detail in the vision, you walked too firmly, so you weren't a ghost after all."

"Jesus," I said. "Now that Branko can't, you'll torment me with ghosts?"

"Oh yes I will," she replied cheerfully. "Your father was lucky to have all these children, and you all carry bits of your father with you wherever you go, and he travels like that in this life with you. He doesn't need to be a ghost. But us poor people who have no children, all we have are ghosts, real ghosts, you know, and that is all we'll be."

"Well, well," I said.

"Will you have some coffee with me?"

"Sure, I love Turkish mud."

She boiled water in a copper pot and sprinkled the black ash of coffee beans into it, and the liquid foamed up brown, smelling like resurrection. We sat down and she slurped and looked out the window to the green Sljeme Mountain and beyond.

"Look at all these clouds," she exclaimed. "Woe to me!"

"What harm can they do? They are beautiful white clouds."

"I used to laugh when Borovnik—remember, Branko talked about him—complained about clouds. He was terrified of them. I found that funny."

"Well, it is. And to be afraid of white clouds is silly."

"They're the worst. All my bones ache, and my hip squeaks. You don't have any broken bones, do you? Just you wait, you'll understand me one day!"

In all the decades before, I must have heard only a dozen sentences from her, but now she seemed to carry the torch of the words of sorrow, and she talked just like Branko did, in his diction, with his relentless zeal. I wanted to close my ears, to fill them with white cotton fluff, when she began to tell me how her husband showed up as a ghost several times, to reassure her that there was life after death, that she should believe. He tends to open the door, pressing down the apartment's door handle and opening it slowly and gently. Usually the door squeaks because my aunt forgets to oil it, but when he opens it, it doesn't squeak at all but glides and opens like the wing of an angel, letting in gentle breezes from the rose garden. Sometimes he touches her shoulder and when she turns around there's only a vanishing blue light in the dark, close to the ceiling.

Her talking like that drove me mad, but I contained my frustrations to rolling my eyes. How could I blame her for believing in ghosts?

Last time I visited her, she dressed in black, combed her thick silver hair, sprinkled perfume on it, and said, "You have a car. Will you drive me to the cemetery? I can't walk very well, I can't take trains. My walking sticks don't support me, I am so unsteady. But I'd love to go to Mirogoj to visit Branko's grave. And it's so beautiful out there, just look at how blue the sky is."

"But why go," I said, "if he visits you?"

"You know, you have a point." She looked at me askance and smiled cleverly. Her eyebrows were black and somehow she looked decades younger. "But I would still like to go to lay the flowers. He loved white roses. I do believe he spends quite a bit of time in his grave, you know."

WINO

The town in which I grew up, Daruvar, was divided along many lines: believers and nonbelievers, communists and anticommunists, Serbs and Croats (and Czechs), but these were all superficial divisions. The really deep and substantial one was between alcoholics and non-alcoholics. I was informed early on that I belonged to the non-alcoholic camp. My father, mother, and siblings—none of them drank. It was a little different with my uncles, one of whom fell off a barn after drinking plum brandy and broke his neck; another kept a vineyard and was always flushed and quiet. In late adolescence, I didn't drink at all, and I abhorred some of my friends who did. I heard they got together, drank beer and brandy, and passed out. Others went to village fairs, had fistfights, got drunk, and had sex with village maidens in haystacks.

Most of these were amateur drunks. A friend of mine, a few years older than me, informed me that alcoholism was a disease, first defined as such, coincidentally, in 1956, my birth year, in the United States. Previously, alcoholism was just a phenomenon. Pop (my friend) explained that there were all sorts of alcoholics, such as rakijasi (brandy drinkers), pivasi (beer drunks), and the worst of all, winos (vinasi). Something in wine made these people hooked and incurable. I didn't know any winos. *Oh, you can recognize them easily,* said Pop. *They dehydrate, so when you see a man drink several glasses of water in the morning, you might look for the correlation of wine in the evening.* Nobody needs to drink water in the morning except alcoholics, he claimed.

It turned out winos were not all that bad. Namely, when I needed to visit Belgrade to take TOEFL (the test of English as a foreign language) so I could apply to American colleges, I asked Pop if he knew where I could crash for the night preceding my test. *No problem,* answered Pop. *I know a wino who has a little house in Zemun, just outside of Belgrade. Misho is his name.*

How do I get in touch with him? I go to the post office and dial him?

Oh no, he's always home. I'll give you the address. Just go there, bang on the door, as he's hard of hearing, and say you are Pop's friend. Give him a one-liter bottle of red wine and you'll be his best friend right away. Maybe he'll be in a good phase, maybe not. His father is an officer, but now and then the police, who hate winos, come over and slap him. For a while they came every morning and woke him up by slapping his face and kicking him. His father probably sent them.

I followed Pop's instructions. It was a snowy, windy February day. I came to a triangular square, found the little house with two shattered windows, and banged on the door. Misho opened the door, tall, disheveled, with somewhat purple undersides to his eyes.

I presented myself, and he laughed, *Josip, like Tito. You must be Croatian, as, though everybody loves Tito in Serbia, nobody names children after him. Oh, and what do I see, a bottle of red.*

Yes, I replied, *Plavac from Peljesac, Zinfandel from the Peljesac peninsula. Pop says I can spend the night here—I have to take tests at the American Embassy tomorrow.*

At the American Embassy! Misho replied. *By all means.*

We sat down and lit a petroleum lamp. *I haven't paid the electric in a year, so the city has cut me off.* The petrol fumes and smoke drifted while Misho popped the bottle open and drank straight from it for a long while, finishing half. *Good, now we can talk,* he said. *If you are tired, you can go right to bed. That down cover is yours for the night.*

I shivered as the snow blew through the windows and the wind whistled cheap melodies over the shards of glass. Misho walked to the cupboard, yanked a glass door open, and took out a handgun.

Do you want to check it out? he asked.

No, I am fine here, I said. *It's really cold; I don't want to leave the bed.*

It's an interesting gadget, he said. *My grandfather had a quarrel one day with my grandma. She was in bed just where you are, in the same bed, at midnight, like now—it's midnight, isn't it?—and he shot her. Yes, my friend, he killed my sweet grandma right there, with three bullets.*

He sobbed and threw the handgun on the floor. He drank more wine. The snow blew through the cracked windows and I shivered.

Would you like a sip? Misho asked. *We need more wine, this is such damned good Croatian wine.*

No, thank you, I replied.

Somehow, at that point I slept. Maybe the secondary lows affected me.

I woke up at dawn, found Misho asleep in the armchair covered by a large green officer's overcoat with a couple of shoulder stripes, probably his grandfather's from World War One. I walked out into the biting wind and caught the bus, and soon I was at the American embassy.

The administrators all smiled, displaying their enviably white teeth, and gave me a B2 pencil to shade the ovals of the correct answers. They all drank water and I eyed them suspiciously.

DUTCH TREAT

"I remember you," said a man in a flower shop at Grand Central as he was about to hand Martin his purchase, a bouquet of red tulips. Martin was reaching for the tulips but the man withdrew them and Martin's right hand clasped the air where the tulips had just been.

"What's that about? I paid."

"You aren't going to get your flowers unless you remember me."

Martin looked at him—bony face, narrowly set small green eyes, slightly crisscrossed. "Sorry, I don't recognize you. I've seen your type of face in the Balkans, though."

"In Srebrenica."

"True. Still, I don't remember your face."

"Maybe you wouldn't. I was a teenager then."

"Teenager?" To Martin, he looked well over thirty. He had silver lines in his black hair, or rather black lines in his silver hair.

"I know what's confusing you. Some of us are aging faster than others."

This encounter evoked memories for Martin, as he left the shop. He used to work for the United Nations in the safe haven of Srebrenica as a sergeant. Even as a child he had admired the UN, and when he went to the States with his father, a banker, they visited the United Nations building. All that glass reflecting the gold of the setting sun struck him as splendid, even more so than the World Trade Center Towers' apparent silverworks. When the Dutch unit was assembled for Bosnia under the auspices of the United Nations, he volunteered. There was not much fighting going on. Most of the massacres had already happened, and most of the houses had already burned down. Well, not completely, since they were built of bricks and cement. So sometimes you'd have a house that looked only slightly charred collapse right in front of you because the wood beams had burned out. The houses were more damaged than they looked, and so were the people. They would go about their business, buying overpriced apples in the marketplace, and then suddenly collapse from a heart attack or stroke.

The UN had deployed units around the town. They were lightly armed, and Martin knew that they couldn't withstand a serious attack. The whole thing was a show. As he walked, he felt like an actor, unconvinced but trying to appear convincing as he strutted, aware of his straight posture, his muscular soccer legs, his curly blond hair, and his firm jaw that kept grinding his complete set of teeth.

The Dutch were given the peculiar task of disarming the local Muslims. They promised protection in exchange for weapons. Muslims brought out hundreds of rifles and pistols, and then the Dutch went house to house, cajoling people to bring out their guns as they searched their basements. The disarmament accomplished, the Dutch UN officers got together with the Serbian officers, and General Mladic drank slivovitz and toasted to "democracy."

Early the next morning, the Serbian military shelled the town. Many houses were on fire. And then the Serb soldiers walked into the town. Martin's unit stayed in the basement of the old gymnasium during the shelling and, afterward, they walked out into the smoky streets. The captain shook hands with a Serbian officer.

"People, don't worry," the announcement came over loud-speakers. "We are looking for a few terrorists, the rest of you are perfectly safe. Just come out, nothing will happen to you. You have a choice, either you can stay here—as you know, this town is very well protected by the Dutch peacekeepers—or move to other towns. Tuzla, Amsterdam, wherever you like."

"Terrorists," Martin asked a Serbian officer. "What are you talking about?"

"Don't pretend to be naïve. Naser Oric and his gang, they've massacred thousands of Serb peasants."

Several dozen Serbian soldiers, dressed as UN Peacekeepers, went around persuading men to come with them to a protected zone. Martin overheard General Krstic say that almost all the men looked like Oric and the boys were probably all Oric's children, and to make sure that they got the terrorist and his accomplices, they had to wipe them all out.

Martin thought the Muslim men would be interrogated, detained for a while, at worst in the way the men had been in the concentration camps of Omarska and Manjaca, with perhaps a dozen murdered. But Manjaca and Omarska had already been disbanded, and the new camps, which were increasing under international scrutiny (more from journalists than the United Nations), couldn't stay in operation for more than a few days. However, the Serbian way of getting around the problem of not being allowed to run detention camps, by slaughtering nearly eight thousand men and boys in one day, was beyond Martin's imagination.

The Dutch soldiers sat impotently and drank and played cards and pretended not to hear the shrieks and the reports that came out of the stadium. Soccer is equal to tulips and windmills as a symbol of Dutch life, and that the Serbs would choose a soccer stadium for this seemed like an additional insult. But what was an insult in the face of mass murder?

The following day, the whole world knew about the Srebrenica massacre. The Dutch peacekeepers were disbanded and shipped back to Holland in disgrace. Their shame became a national shame, and eventually the Dutch government had to resign over the scandal of supplying sham peacekeepers as accomplices to genocide.

Martin quit his nascent military career and began to study religion, and now he was spending a year at the Union Theological seminary as a Fulbright scholar. He often wondered whether he could have done anything differently and whether there was anything he could have done after the war to atone for what had happened, and now all that emotional and historical baggage hit him in the face of the exhausted-looking young man who had sold him the red tulips.

Martin returned to the shop the next day. "Let's have a drink when you're done with work," he offered the Bosnian behind the counter.

"A Dutch treat?"

"No, not in that sense," said Martin. "I'll treat."

"So, it's a Dutch treat." The way the Bosnian pronounced it, it sounded like the Dutch threat.

"If you like."

"I never thought I'd want to talk to another Dutchman, especially you, but okay. By the way, my name is Esad." They shook hands. Esad's hand was limp, cool, and sweaty. Instead of becoming firmer as Martin pumped it in a hearty rhythm, it grew even limper. They went across the street to a huge bar, an arcade under the Park Avenue Bridge into Grand Central. Martin ordered Grolsch.

"You know, we could talk about other things but I'll still be thinking of that day," said Esad, "so I might just as well tell you how it was for me. UN soldiers came to our house. At least we thought they were UN soldiers. Many of them were blond so that fit the picture. I was surprised to hear them speak Serbian. They said they would put us on the buses and take us to Split on the Adriatic. That sounded pretty nice to me, and I wanted to believe their story. As a boy, I used to spend one month every summer in Omis near Split, in a recreation camp for railway workers. My father was a rail worker." Esad paused and his eyes grew shiny as he cleared his throat. "You know what fear smells like?"

"Like what?"

"Not like tulips."

"Well, I have my ideas, but tell me yours."

"Like piss."

"Well, that can be."

"Sure, when you walk into a public men's room, you always feel uneasy because of that smell. Piss is the territory marker for wild animals, to tell others, now be afraid if you cross this line. New York smells to me like fear; wherever I turn, there's that smell of urine. This is how I learned to read the smell: I was taken out into the soccer field with my father and brothers. We were shouted at and beaten. I fell in the mud, and as I tried to get up, somebody fell over me. The shots after that sounded soft and muffled because I heard them through the bodies piled over me. It was all urine and blood then, dying men and boys releasing their bladders. I couldn't breathe with all the weight on top of me, and so I passed out. Later when I woke up, I was no longer buried and the stars were shining. I imagined the bodies were being taken away to be buried, and there were just a few of us left scattered. I crawled away, afraid that I would be noticed and shot. My clothes were soaked, blood, shit, and urine. I didn't know whether some of it was mine, it probably was. It's an experience I'll never forget. You had to be there. Oh, I forgot, you were there. You were warm, drinking your Ballantine's, and enjoying the new crop of Bosnian jokes. Tell me what jokes were you retelling that evening to kill the time?"

"Believe me, there were no jokes. We were all in shock. Who would've thought?"

"We had. But you didn't listen to us."

After three bottles of Grolsch, Martin said, "You know, you're such a wonderful guy. I'm so glad to have met you."

"It would be better if I'd never met you."

"I mean now, not then."

"It's okay to talk, but talk is filthy cheap. It doesn't do much, it doesn't change anything."

"It changes nothing in the past, but we have a whole future. You are a young man, how can you talk like that?"

"When you have something that big in your past, you don't think of the future. There's no future that won't contain that past."

"Come on, cheer up. I too feel terrible about what happened but I wasn't in command. I was simply obeying orders and I didn't know."

"I don't know what you didn't know. I'm not accusing you."

"Where do you live?"

"In Astoria."

"How can you afford rent when you sell flowers? That can't bring in much."

"It's not all I do, but I still can't pay this month's rent, or last month's rent. They'll evict me soon. Worse things could happen. How should I care?"

Martin banged the table. His fist hurt. He used to do karate and was supposed to be able to slice bricks with his hand but that was a while back. His hand has grown soft. He shook his hand in front of him as though it had been burnt.

Esad laughed. "What are you doing?"

"I've just had an idea. Can I give you ten thousand dollars, to help you with rent and dental work?"

"Dental work? You don't like my teeth? They are yellow from too much tobacco, but there's not a single cavity in them. Anyway, don't tease me with money."

"I'm serious. It would make me feel better."

"You probably feel pretty good anyway."

"It's the least I could do in the way of apology."

"And to your mind that would be that. Ten thousand, and you'd feel better."

"That's all I can afford. That's half of my fellowship. I'm not rich. What would you like me to do?"

"I don't think you can do anything to right the wrong. Can you resurrect people?"

"I wish I could. I study resurrection."

"What's there to study? Can you kill people?"

"No."

"You've proved that you can by helping the killers. The best thing, even better than resurrection, would be if you could go to Bosnia and find Mladic and kill him."

"How could I do that? Look at all these people, you included, who need revenge. If you can't do it, how could I?"

"You partied with him. You guys are on good terms."

"And you'd feel better if he were shot?"

"Much better."

"He'll probably end up in Den Hague." Martin pronounced the Hague in his native, gutteral way.

"Kharrkh," echoed Esad, clearing his throat. He stuck out his tongue with green spittle on it and then spat. His spittle flew like a bullet and hit the dark varnished floor.

Martin looked around, afraid that someone might have seen the spitting. The waitress, who looked like a ballerina with her hair bobbed, promptly walked toward them; she slid over the spittle but easily regained her balance. She asked Martin, "Is everything all right, sir? Would you like another beer?"

"Maybe in five minutes."

"May I touch your hair?" she said. "I always wanted to have such curly hair."

Martin blushed while she petted him as though he were a sheep. His scalp tingled pleasantly.

"Khargh won't do any good." Esad cleared his throat but didn't spit. "He'll be nicely fed, get the best doctors to take care of his heart and kidneys, and maybe he'll get thirty years of good retirement. That International War Crimes Tribunal, why is it in Holland? Instead of handing over the mass murderers to us in Sarajevo to shoot, you coddle them. And you know what, even your beer is overrated. The Belgians who you treat like peasants and scum make much better beer."

Martin watched the waitress at the bar as she tilted her hips, exposing her bumpy knees.

"Sure, if it makes you feel better to put down the country, go ahead."

"The whole world knows that you are all stingy."

Martin pulled his checkbook out of his blazer pocket. "I'll write you a check."

"I'm not challenging you. Actually, I don't have a bank account."

"With this, you could open one. How can you live without a bank account?"

"Better than with one. I wouldn't know how to get a bank account."

"Let's go to the bank, and we'll open one."

"But that takes all sorts of papers."

"Just a few."

"I have none on me. I don't believe in papers. I don't want to be in this government's records, I don't want to be tracked by any government."

"How can you avoid that? You have passports, and when you got your refugee status, which you must have after '95, you're registered in many places."

"I'm not a refuse."

"Refugee."

"Same thing. I'm not an exile, I'm not a citizen. I'm nothing."

"How did you get here?"

"That's a long story."

"I'd love to hear it."

"I don't feel like telling it. Plus, it would turn out to be a story. I would make things up."

"Why?"

"I don't want anybody to know the truth. Truth can harm you, lies can't. Well, are you serious about giving me all that money?"

"That's the least I can do to assuage this feeling of guilt."

"I'd do you a favour if I took your dirty money, is that it?"

Esad laughed, and his body shook the table, rattling its knives and forks and causing the fresh pints of Grolsch to foam. "What a way to think! You don't owe me anything. You are nothing, like me. How could you owe me anything?"

"I just do."

"Are you sure you won't regret this?"

"Why would I?"

"You never know. You probably will. Can you give it to me in cash?"

"The banks are closed now. It's after four. I could come back tomorrow and give you the cash."

"I'm not going to be here tomorrow. And I don't want to see you again."

"Why?" Martin was hurt. "I thought we were making friends."

"Maybe we are. Most of my friends I won't ever see again, so you'd fit right in."

Martin shuddered because he didn't know what to make of that. "Tell you what. We can go to the bank, and I'll give you $500 cash. That's the max I can draw from Citibank. I'll write you a check for the rest."

Martin scribbled a check for Esad and left a ten-dollar tip on the table. They walked down the block to a Citibank glassed-in cash machine lobby. The cash popped out with a hiss and a click from the mouth of the automaton, in fresh fifty-dollar bills, which still smelled of printing dyes. Esad winked, took the bills, and placed them in a thin pigskin wallet. The skin of the wallet was shiny from being worn in the back pocket.

"Would you like to see my pictures?"

"Sure," said Martin.

Esad showed several men with thin moustaches and small eyes. "My father. Dead, you know. Uncle, dead, of known causes. Older brother, same thing."

"How about your mother, sisters?"

"They're alive."

"You don't carry their pictures?"

"No, I don't believe in keeping pictures of the living. I carry only the male line, all dead, my private ghosts. They give me strength."

"Strength for what?"

"To dream. To have visions."

"Visions of what?"

Esad's eyes shone, accumulating tears that wouldn't spill over but would stay there, growing brilliant in the glare of the sun, which reflected from the glass across the street, from the Grace building, casting light over Bryant Park. The low light radiated off the large sycamore leaves bending their heads contritely toward Esad, as though worshipping his grief, or saying goodbye to him, vermilion in their beautiful shame.

"Thank you, my friend," said Esad. He turned and walked away toward the BDF lines subway entrance alongside the NY Public Library, next to the ornate little restroom hut from which wafted smells of male imprecision.

"Wait!" Martin shouted. "Give me your phone number or email so we can stay in touch."

"I don't do email, and my phone is disconnected. I can't keep a phone, I talk too much. Couldn't keep up with the bills."

"Maybe now you could?"

"Oh, I have other expenses and other bad habits. Plus, don't you think all the phones are bugged?"

"Tell you what, let's meet at the Starbucks on the corner of Sixth and Forty-Second, the day after tomorrow, at four. I'd like to talk more."

"I don't see why. OK, if you wish." Esad walked into the subway entrance.

Martin watched him; Esad's walk was stiff, as though his spine had been broken, and his thick silvery hair shone, and even after he'd vanished down the stairs into the dark, Martin saw that silver light lingering in the entrance. He blinked, but it was still there.

Martin walked to Eighth Avenue, to the A line. A man in rags slept upside down on the stairs. Huge rats were leaping over the tracks. So, this was New Amsterdam? Just to think of it, this used to be all Dutch. On the train, he fidgeted as the hard plastic seemed to shut off his blood circulation, sending his left leg into tingling sleep. What happened to our influence, thought Martin. We owned this place, the ground on which the UN building stands, and where are we now? Who listens to us? We try to listen to everybody, learn all these languages, and what good does it all do?

He entered his apartment on the second floor above a dry cleaner's shop, on 207th Street. There was a chemical smell, and he couldn't isolate it with his nostrils—formaldehyde? Acetone? He was sure the fumes were coming from the shop, through the creaking floor. If mice could crawl through some spacing in the floor, then the fumes could too.

He placed the tulips from the day before, which were still in their paper wrapping, into a blue vase and poured tap water into a pot. He waited for the chlorine haze in the water to clear and then filled up the vase. The tulips perked up and stood straight, like little kings.

———

Two days later, while waiting for Esad, Martin drank two cappuccinos, enjoying the steam and foam. Esad didn't show up. Martin went to the entrance of Grand Central, and there were no flowers being sold there anymore. No Esad. Never mind, maybe tomorrow. He went to the bar and looked around to see the waitress (maybe she'd be free for a drink?) but she wasn't there.

He checked his bank balance to see whether Esad had withdrawn the money. For no reason at all, he looked up at the surveillance camera in the high right corner of the room, with its red light blinking, recording, and that made him self-conscious. Is there someone watching me right now? His balance was still over twelve thousand. Apparently, Esad hadn't cashed the check yet. Maybe two days wasn't enough time to open an account and cash such a large amount.

A week later, the check hadn't gone through yet.

Martin's tulips were waning. Well, how long can you live on water alone? They lived anyway, like prisoners of Martin's nostalgia. Their necks drooped more than ever, as though they were looking for something spilled and lost.

Maybe they smelled the fumes from the ground floor as well, from the gas chamber that was used to keep people looking clean and sharp and starched.

The noxious chemical smell kept Martin awake and burned his sinuses.

In the morning, he staggered down to the shop under the pretext of having his blazer cleaned. The man behind the counter was small and thin and gray, his cheeks drawn. No doubt, that's what happens when you are exposed to chemicals for a long time, thought Martin.

"By the way," Martin said, "What chemical process are you using here? I live right above you, and the fumes from here are terrible."

"What fumes? I can't smell anything."

"*You* wouldn't. You live with them."

"Can you smell anything here?"

"Your machines are in the back."

"I have no machines. We actually have all our stuff dry cleaned in our twin store, two blocks down on Broadway."

"But all the chemicals stay in the clothes and they rise straight into my apartment."

"You are imagining things, my friend. Come back here and sniff if you want to."

Martin did, and he had to admit that there was not much chemical smell there.

Later that day, he saw Esad coming out of an electronics store on Avenue of the Americas. There was a glow around him, as though he'd plugged into an electronic device. Martin followed him in the street, and when Esad turned around, Martin waved, but Esad apparently didn't see him, or if he did, he pretended not to. He walked so fast that Martin thought of running to catch up, but it was a hot and humid summer day. Down the avenue, the hot air danced, refracting images and leaving illusory oil puddles on the pavement, which dissolved and evaporated when Martin approached them. Esad went into the subway, and Martin broke into a run after all, just managing to squeeze through the closing doors of the Q train. He wanted to go to the other car but the train door was locked. At the next stop, Martin went to the other coach where Esad had been but couldn't spot him there. Did Esad change cars too? At every stop, Martin stepped out the doors to look down the platform, but he didn't see Esad exit. Martin got off at the last stop in Astoria, and there was still no Esad on the platform. Martin was terribly thirsty, sweating, dizzy. Maybe there was no Esad? Maybe there was never an Esad, and I've imagined this whole thing all the way along? That would explain why the check never got cashed. Maybe I never wrote it.

Am I losing my mind? This damned city, with all its chemical smells and noises and light. Oh no, it can't be, nothing that convincing and vivid would have happened as a figment of my imagination. He still felt the limpid handshake in his fist, all too real, fleshly.

For several days in a row, Martin took the Q train, hoping to run into Esad. He was mad at himself for having been so lackadaisical the day he saw Esad not to run after him at the first instance. It would have been nice to talk to Esad, to get an update, and to figure out in what other ways he could help. As long as Esad didn't cash his check, Martin would be in suspense, like the families of the dead whose corpses are missing and can't be buried. Now he understood the need for corporeal evidence and closure. If he ever saw Esad again, he'd have to give him a hug, squeeze him, make sure he was all there, not just a hallucination of an overproductive conscience.

Almost every night, Martin had dreams about Esad. In one, they were playing soccer, using a severed head with a thin moustache as a ball. Esad kicked it and Martin flew to catch it, but couldn't quite reach, and the head slid over the tips of his fingers and into the net. Martin woke up from that nightmare with a terrible headache. The fumes were on again in his apartment. He decided to sniff from one corner to the other on all fours, to see where the smell was coming from. It was most intense below the artificial Persian rug in the center of the room. Martin moved the rug to locate the leaking cracks better, but the smell diminished. He concluded that the smell must be coming out of the carpet itself, and so he folded the carpet and put it in the closet. Now that noxious smell no longer permeated the apartment. How simple! He was proud of himself for eliminating the problem. He changed the sheets and enjoyed their coolness.

He fell asleep and dreamed that he and Esad were wrestling naked. When Martin gripped him, Esad slipped away. And when Esad gripped him by the neck, his oily hands couldn't hold on, and Martin slipped out of the grip. Martin gripped him again, and found that instead of trying to knock each other to the ground, they held each other's penises firmly. Esad's hand on his was warm and rough; Martin could feel the calluses, some of them jagged and prickly like glass, maybe they were glass. Martin woke up. He was surprised that it was only a dream and noticed that he had a hard-on. He was disappointed that it was a dream—he would have loved to see Esad again, but probably not like that. He didn't think he had any gay impulses.

In the morning, a little embarrassed, he didn't go out to look for Esad. He pondered whether he was actually attracted to Esad. Or was it all just historical, abstract, ethical, an attraction of his conscience to the wronged party? But what if it all was simple, obscenely physical, and all that history and theology just a smokescreen?

A month later, the check went through. Esad Hajiabdic, the name said.

There was no phone number on the check, but there was an address on Queens Boulevard. Martin went there and rang the bell, but there was no answer. He waited for hours outside the house, all in vain.

Two months after he saw Esad outside the electronics shop, the planes flew into the World Trade Center.

Martin took a bus and walked to see the destructive miracle. Besides feeling horror, he adored the sight of all the smoke, as though witnessing the epiphany of an angry God. His throat went dry from excitement, or perhaps from the association of ideas, of smoke and thirst. He went to a deli to get some orange juice, and there he watched on TV as the second tower came crumbling down. The two Arabic-looking men who ran the shop didn't want to charge him anything for the juice, and said, "That's on us. How would a dollar make any difference on a day like this?" They smiled, their eyes glowing, barely containing their joy.

Martin smiled too as he watched the tower go down, and when he saw how happy the men were, he laughed for a few seconds, but once he left the shop he felt queasy. The dark cloud was spreading. Past him walked men and women with ashes in their hair and on their clothes, their eyes large from fear. They looked like pilgrims on Ash Wednesday. Seeing their fear, Martin grew terrified, too.

And when he saw the running electronic sign at Times Square post a figure, maybe ten thousand people dead, he felt no Schadenfreude, just sorrow. But he remembered that he had felt Schadenfreude in the shop and wondered about what he actually wanted, who he was, and what demons were inside him. Maybe he wouldn't have been so desperate for forgiveness from Esad if he hadn't imagined that there was evil in him.

He had to wait for a few hours before the subway would run again. He didn't know whether another plane would crash at Times Square, or whether there would be a nuclear bomb exploding, and in the subway he looked around at the bags, and there were many, maybe from Penn Central and Port Authority. What if a bomb went off? He was surprised—and obliquely almost let down—that no bombs went off.

The following day he went to Queens again, rang the bell, but got no answer. On the way back, Martin wondered again about all the bags in the train. How come they go off in Jerusalem and Istanbul and many other cities and not in New York? Wasn't that merely a matter of time?

A huge man stood in front of him in the A train. He kept looking glassily at Martin. His gaze grew more and more annoying, and Martin walked to another car at 125th. He sat down, but as he looked up, he saw the same man staring at him. It was as though Martin hadn't shifted from the first car. Martin stood up and walked back to the first car, but the giant followed him.

Martin looked at him with animosity, trying to browbeat him, but the man smiled lovingly, revealing a whole row of gold teeth.

Any other expression on the man's face would have made sense to Martin, but this appearance of liquid love seemed cynical, creepy, invasive, threatening. Martin shuddered.

Martin walked to the other end of the car, and the giant followed.

Am I being stalked? thought Martin.

Until now, he couldn't understand why stalking was so highly rated as a threat in the States, why it was treated as a crime, and why so many women complained about it. When he was a boy and he liked a girl, he'd follow her, just to admire her for a few blocks. Even later he saw that as a normal kind of imprinting behavior, where you follow your infatuation impulses unabashedly like a helpless duckling.

Martin jumped off the train at 175th even though it wasn't his stop. He felt the big presence looming behind him and quickened his pace, but when he turned around, there was nobody there. With relief, he slowed his pace and walked up the stairs, and then back down to catch the next train.

Now he wasn't sure that there had been a man stalking him on the previous train. New York is merciless that way, it can give you illusions, he thought. He'd forgotten to eat all day, and with the coffee and beer he'd drunk, he'd reached a stage of weakness and dizziness.

Three months after he saw Esad outside the electronics store, Martin was in the subway when it slowed down near Chambers Street. Nobody spoke in the train car. The doors didn't open at Chambers Street, and the train inched along. There were many white tulips and white carnations laid out on the platform. Martin wished he could contribute. Maybe he'd have to find out how—he could buy tulips, ideally red ones from Esad, and then lay them down on the platform. He had a sensation of shuddering grief at the sight of his national flowers, little Dutch souls in New Amsterdam trying to do some good in their lame and lovable way.

Even at home, he couldn't get rid of the sensation of sadness. But worse than sadness was that terrible smell from the destroyed World Trade Center—a mix of concrete dust, burnt plastic, the suggestion of flesh, human flesh, and perhaps burnt hair wafting through the windows. For days he'd been encountering that smell everywhere, as the winds blew mostly from the south, along the island, and somehow it was similar to the old smell from his Persian carpet, which he'd taken out and left on the sidewalk next to an improvised shrine with pictures of people from the neighbourhood who'd perished in the towers, with flags everywhere, small ones glued to the shrine, large ones draping from the windows on the yellow-bricked building across the street.

To wash away the tragic smell and the sweat of the city, Martin took a shower. He thought he heard some pounding on the door, but he ignored it because it could have been coming from somewhere else. But when he stepped out and wrapped a towel around his torso, he was startled by three cleanly dressed men in black shoes with thick rubber soles. "What are you doing here? Who the hell are you?"

"Mr. Neeskens, you're coming with us."

"What's this all about?" Martin asked. "You broke into my apartment! You broke the law."

"We'll see who broke the law. Come with us, calmly."

"Why would I?"

"You'll find out in due time. We need you to help us with some information gathering."

He was fingerprinted, all his papers were photocopied, scrutinized, and his body was searched a little more thoroughly than Martin found comfortable.

"Just a routine procedure, sir."

"But why?"

"You'll find out when we gather enough evidence. Anyway, you know why. You tell me why."

"I have no idea."

"It's about your financing the terrorists."

"What an outrageous idea! I didn't finance any terrorists. Where do you come up with such nonsense?"

"Don't pretend. We know more than you think we do, so you're better off telling us the truth."

"This is all rather mysterious to me. You have confused me with someone else."

"Now, tell us what Muslims you know."

"Not many. There aren't many in my field, Christian theology."

"You worked for the UN in Bosnia, and you made plenty of contacts with the local Muslims and quite possibly with the foreign fighters, the Mujahideen. We need to know how it all worked out."

"How what worked out? You know that Bosnian Muslims couldn't possibly be involved in this American tragedy. Overall, they love America. America saved them. They see you as saviours."

"Maybe that's not how everybody there saw us."

"From what I could tell…"

"Let's get straight to the point. You wrote a check for $9,500 to a certain Esad Hajiabdic, who wrote a check in the amount of $9,000 to Atta as soon as your check cleared. Atta cashed it in Germany, bought several airfares, and flew into a World Trade Center tower. Now, clearly Esad was merely a middleman you used to finance the terrorists."

"My God, what a strange story!"

"Yes, it is, you have some explaining to do."

He retold them the story of his being a peacekeeper in Srebrenica who felt guilty for what had happened and wanted to make small amends, such as he could, by helping Esad. "And by the way, why are you sure Esad was involved? Maybe he merely bought a car from Atta, or something like that, and paid with a check."

One investigator laughed. "You want us to buy your sob story?"

"That's the simple truth."

"And the not-so-simple truth is that you've come to this country to subvert it, working for Al Qaeda."

"That's outrageous!" exclaimed Martin. "I need a lawyer."

"Probably you were another middleman. Nothing will happen to you if you didn't know what was going on. Maybe you were simply used, but we need to know by whom, and how. You want to save people? You can. Give us the information about how the network works. Who gave you the money?"

For several days he was interrogated in a New Jersey prison, and he stayed there in a solitary cell for three months, with nothing to do, going out of his mind. The smell of cement and some unidentifiable gases irritated him, as did the absence of daylight and his not knowing what time of day or night it was. He was perpetually thirsty and hungry, and the cement dust hovering around him like a galaxy of sinking and remote stars, that had lost their light made his throat parched. Several times he was woken up out of deep sleep to be interrogated and, on one occasion, the principal investigator—a heavyset man with a bristly moustache who constantly sweated—said to him, "You know, we were thinking of letting you go. You're an honorable UN soldier, and something like this could have happened without your actually being involved. I could buy your story, but look what we just saw on a surveillance camera tape, recorded on 9/11. Look at this. At the time the towers were collapsing, you were in a Palestinian grocery store, where a couple of hijackers had been videotaped several weeks before. See, there you are, looking happy, cheering as the towers go down! It's too much of a coincidence for us to let it go unquestioned—way too many 'coincidences.'"

BE PATIENT

In 1952, one midmorning in Daruvar, Croatia, Doctor Maric held up the injection with a thin needle, which gleamed in the beam of the morning sun. He held it up as though aiming for the sky and said, "This is a wonderful thing. It won't hurt at all, and it will prevent your children from getting the measles."

"They stick a needle into you?" asked Lyerka. "I'm scared of needles."

"It won't hurt at all," Nenad, her father, replied.

"How do you know?"

"I've had lots of those when I was sick."

A boy in front of them cried.

"So why is he crying?"

"From fear, not pain," explained the doctor.

"I won't cry," she said.

When the doctor pushed in the needle, Lyerka's dark brown eyes grew wet, but she didn't let out a sound. A couple of brilliant tears welled along her long eyelashes.

"Now, that's my girl," said Nenad.

A nurse rubbed alcohol over the puncture and covered it with gauze, and said, "Hold it there for a while."

Lyerka did. A scarlet spot of blood appeared on the gauze.

"You have a beautiful girl," the nurse said to Nenad.

"I know. I don't know what I did to deserve such beauty."

"Oh, you know what you did! We all deserve beauty, but few of us get it."

"You have nothing to complain of."

Nenad noticed her deft long fingers, and he admired her blond hair, curving forward over her ears. It wasn't real blond, but chemical, and it complemented her dark blue eyes.

"Oh, thank you! It's so rare in socialism to get a compliment. It's a bourgeois manner."

"Life is too sad not to indulge in little pleasantries," he retorted.

Heading out the door, Nenad paused to check out the nurse's form as she leaned over to put the needle into a candle flame—very thin waist and wide hips.

"Tata, have you forgotten something?" asked Lyerka.

"No."

"Why is she burning the needle? So it will hurt more?"

"So nobody will get sick. Fire kills the germs."

He held Lyerka's hand and admired how small it was in his big fist. His hand had been enlarged through too much work and appetite, which he'd inherited from his father, who had basically eaten himself to death. At least he managed to die before World War II. There was a blessing there, at least for him.

Lyerka skipped steps over the cobbles in the town center, past a rusty hot water fountain, and they walked into an ice cream parlor. "You took it so well, my sweetie, you deserve a little strawberry ice cream."

She licked it, sticking out her little red tongue, like a kitten licking milk.

"How do you feel?"

"Good. It's nice to be taking a walk with you."

"I know. I am usually too busy to do this, but I promise we'll do it every day."

Lyerka smiled wide. "But no more needles," she said.

"You didn't like it, of course. Does it still hurt?"

"No. It's fine. It just itches a little."

"No worse than a bee sting?"

"Much better."

A stray dog, with long hanging ears, came up to Lyerka, and Lyerka petted him. The dog blinked and licked her hand.

"See, he loves me."

"He loves the ice cream sticking to your fingers. But yes, he loves you; everybody does."

She lifted one of his hanging ears and petted it.

"Don't touch him. He could have all sorts of diseases."

"Could we take him home?"

"No. Where would he stay?"

"You could build him a doghouse. It's easy for you; you can build anything."

Nenad laughed. "Yes, a doghouse I could, but I don't see why. Plus, the dog is bigger than you. What if he has rabies? He could bite you."

"He won't. He likes me. Look at him." She buried her little fingers in the dog's long orange hairs.

Nenad pulled her by the hand, away from the dog.

"That hurts, Daddy! That's my sore arm."

"I didn't know it was sore. Sorry, we have to get home."

She didn't say anything. The dog followed a few paces behind. She turned around. "He wants to come with us. Look at those big eyes! He's crying."

"Dogs can't cry."

The dog furrowed his brows, and there were creases on his forehead; he looked worried and thoughtful.

"Don't look at him," Nenad said. "That encourages him."

"But why can't I have a dog?"

"We have enough cats running around our yard."

"They're all wild, and I can't pet them."

"At least you learned that lesson when that nasty tomcat nearly scratched your eye out."

"Oh, he was just scared. He's nice now that I bring out some leftovers."

"I didn't know we had leftovers."

At home, Marta had just brought in a pile of scrap wood in a pleated basket from the workshop. "You all look ruddy and fresh," she said.

"The walk did us good. The sun is strong, and the wind from the mountains is chilly. And to talk with Lyerka means happiness, you know."

"There's a letter for you, from the taxation office." She pointed to a blue envelope with a stamp. Nenad checked out the stamp: the walled city of Dubrovnik. He used to collect stamps.

"Why are you staring at the envelope? The letter is inside; won't you read it? They want you to pay more taxes."

"Of course, when did they want me to pay less? Bastards, they won't let a decent man live."

"I suppose they're just doing their job. You don't want to end up in jail, do you?"

"I'm not afraid of their jails. I've been to worse places in the war. Now, of course I'll go pay, but how am I going to feed our growing family?"

"We're doing fine, praise the Lord."

"Yes, the Lord and me."

"Are you all hungry?"

Marta, a solid woman with a thin nose and small green eyes beneath a tall forehead, prepared palachinkas for supper. She put cottage cheese with a bit of sugar inside the crepes and offered them to their children.

Pretty soon there was a measured triple knock on the thick oak door, and Nenad's stocky brother Drago, endowed with emphatically upturned black eyebrows, came in with his sensationally pale and nearly translucent wife, Maria. There was no phone in the entire town, and if people wanted to visit, they came directly over, risking being turned away if the family was busy. But after darkness gathered hardly anybody worked, although most of them fussed, canning and pickling peppers or dancing on their bleeding grapes or on sliced cabbage or reading old yellow-papered novels. Nobody had TV sets, and guests were in demand as a source of entertainment.

Marta brought out tablecloths to adorn the otherwise naked aged wood. The pale beechwood resembled human flesh in hue, and to her it seemed indecent; it would have to be covered for the visitors. There were a few grease stains from duck soup, a burn mark from a brimming-hot frying pan off the stove, and a few scars from children's cutting with knives. There were lots of knives all over the house and in the workshop, where Nenad made tables and chairs for a living.

"Would you like some rose hip tea?" Marta offered. "We also have some white wine. My husband no longer drinks anything alcoholic. His doctor tells him it's best not to."

"Oh, doctors," Drago answered. "They always tell you what not to do, but it would be better if they told you what to do. Yes, I'll have a glass of wine."

"And so will I," said his blue-eyed wife, Maria. She was half German, half Czech. After the last world war, her parents were driven out like many Germans, and that Maria could remain had to do with her being married to Drago, who had to his credit killing four ambushed German soldiers.

Drago drew a loud gulp of greenish wine, exceedingly sour and tart. "Strange days—suddenly we can't talk about Mother Russia anymore, and America is our new friend."

"Politics, they always change, it's best not to talk about it," Marta said.

"Why not?" Nenad said. "You can't spend your life in fear that something bad will happen. A lot of bad stuff happened, and a lot more will, but we can at least talk about it."

"We're getting all sorts of modern help from America," said Drago, "better antibiotics, better radios, better beans. Can you believe it? Serbian beans, pasulj, for years came from America."

"I know, and today our children were inoculated against the measles," Nenad said. "Yugoslavia is the first country in the world to get the medicine!"

"That's strange," Maria said. "Why don't they use it in America first?"

"They don't have a crisis like we do."

"It's not a crisis," Drago said. "You get it, and so what? A few spots, a fever."

"Maybe you are thinking of rubella. This is rubeola. The high fevers can damage your heart."

"Oh, everything can damage your heart. You don't brush your teeth right, or you sleep on the wrong side; you spend too much time in bed or too little; you work too hard or too little, and your heart fails."

"Americans are nice to us," Marta said.

"Well, the American friendship is all self-interest," Drago said. "It's military propaganda to keep us away from the Soviet bloc."

"I don't care about the motives as long as the deeds are good," said Nenad. "Lyerka, apple of my eye, will you play a song for our guests?"

Lyerka, dressed in white, glowed. She could pick a few melodies on the piano, and she improvised, in the right key, "Ave Maria." She stood in her tiny clogs next to the piano, dancing slowly while choosing the keys.

"Beautiful, isn't she?" said Marta, her mother.

Upon hearing the compliment, Lyerka smiled, and her eyes seemed to grow in size. Dimples appeared on her flushed and round cheeks. The blackness of her hair transcended itself into flickers of blue.

"She's smart too," Marta said. "Ask her to multiply numbers, and see what happens."

"What is seven times seven?" asked Drago.

"Almost fifty," she answered.

"What do you mean by almost fifty?"

"Forty-nine."

"And what is nine times nine?"

"Just a little over eighty."

"Bravo!" Maria said. "And she's only five?"

"Almost five!" answered Lyerka.

Marta took off her scarf, shook her curly hair, which sprang up. She tied it into a tall bun. Her life was fulfilled. She had a clever and curious son who wanted to become a journalist, an older daughter who liked to read the encyclopedia, and now she had a brilliant little girl who would grow up to be a music teacher or even perhaps a doctor. In socialism, women could study like men, and since they weren't drunks you could foretell their future.

For the evening meal, Marta prepared žganci, a hot corn cereal with fresh cow milk. Lyerka tiptoed to the stove, where a pot of boiled milk was cooling off and forming a wrinkled cover of cream. She scooped it up in a soup spoon, which in her tiny hand looked like a ladle. While Lyerka chewed the cream, looking beatific, Marta said, "You should never walk barefoot; where are your clogs? You'll catch a cold!"

Nenad said grace, and at the end of the meal he kissed everybody goodnight. He was making sure they would have an orderly life, something he hadn't experienced in his upbringing, where his father, damaged by World War I and captivity in Russia, had a bad temper. He couldn't control his appetite because he had spent four years starving in Siberia. Every meal to him seemed to be the last one, so he devoured as much as possible, with lots of feferoni, yet he was thin, stringy, and fiery.

The following day, after a lunch of bread, milk, and honey, Lyerka scratched her arm.

Nenad asked, "It hurts?"

"Tata, it still itches."

"But it doesn't hurt?"

"No. Could I have a glass of water? I'm thirsty."

"Can't you get it for yourself?"

"You're right, I am just a little tired."

"Fine, I'll get you a glass." He poured the water from a bucket on a chair. They had no indoor plumbing; Marta had brought in a bucket drawn from their spindle well.

Lyerka gulped the water greedily.

"She's kind of red in the face," said Marta.

"A bit flushed from the wind. She went out to look for the cats. The last gasp of winter, it's energizing."

Marta felt Lyerka's forehead. "She's warm."

"They say it's normal. After the shot, you can run a slight fever for three days."

"Strange idea, to take healthy children to the hospital and give them fevers in the name of health."

"That's good planning, and Americans are great at that. They've knocked out TB, and now they'll get rid of most diseases."

"What are we going to die of then?"

"Old age."

"I'm sleepy. Can I go to bed?" asked Lyerka.

"But it's the middle of the day, and you're too old for naptime."

"She's not too old," Nenad said. "Spaniards do it all their lives."

Marta said, "We should give her some aspirin."

"It's not fever, only a slight temperature rise. Perfectly normal."

"It would be normal to keep it down."

"I think it's good for the body to learn how to fight off fevers. Probably the inoculation works better with the heat—the body is producing antibodies. It's like a little foundry. Foundries are always hot. Fire kills the germs." He closed his eyes and saw the needle in the flame held by deft, elongated fingers.

"I'll give her some lemonade at least." Marta took out a lemon, sliced it in half, and squeezed it into a glass.

"It's great that our country is making friends in Africa," Nenad said, "so we can have lemons. How old were you when you had your first lemon? I had mine in 1935. We didn't know that there was a difference between lemons and yellow pears, so we ate the skins too and wondered how such a bitter and sour fruit could be so popular."

"Thanks, Mama. My throat is dry and scratchy. Can I have more?"

Marta felt Lyerka's forehead.

"Jesus, you're burning up! Where's the thermometer? Nenad, come over here, she's all red. She's shivering. My God, she's in trouble. Take her to the clinic right away!"

Nenad tried to place her on the bicycle in the child-carrying seat, but she couldn't sit up straight.

"She's too weak to sit up, and I don't think she has any sense of balance," he said. "I better carry her."

As he walked up the cobbles on the hill, he sweated. Her heat was getting to him; he panted.

At the clinic, the doctor on duty smoked a cigar and asked, "Fever and you get excited? Children have fevers all the time." His moustache was gray and white, vertical white stripes, except under the nose, where they were yellow, black and yellow. But as he looked at Lyerka, he said, "You're right, she looks too hot."

A black-haired nurse, who also had a moustache, put the thermometer under Lyerka's tongue. Lyerka's chin shook. The doctor felt her neck below her ears. "Her glands are a little too swollen."

"What is it?" asked Nenad.

"An allergic reaction to the inoculation. Probably nothing serious, but we have to drive her to the hospital right away. We have one more child with high fever and neck swelling like that, and they're already waiting for the car downstairs."

The ambulance drove over potholes in town and then over the mud and gravel to the hospital in Pakrac, twenty-two kilometers away. The ambulance thudded on the wooden bridge over the river Pakra. The hospital was painted all blue.

A father and his son, the same age as Lyerka, went through the doors first. The son was shivering violently, and he moaned more than Lyerka did.

Nenad and his daughter waited in a dark corridor.

"Can't they turn on the lights?" asked Nenad.

"No, we have to save on electricity," said a cleaning woman dressed in dark blue and sweeping, raising the dust, which accumulated from crumbs of caked soil slipping out from underneath people's soles.

Lyerka moaned and then coughed.

"Will you stop sweeping dust and germs right into our mouths?"

"No, I can't. A job is a job. It has to be done."

"Do it when we're gone."

"Most people are gone."

"Don't you see the child is coughing?"

"It's a hospital. Everybody is coughing. What do you expect?"

"Get out of our way, you smart fatass!"

"Don't become abusive, comrade. Who do you think you are?"

But when Nenad stood up and swore colorfully (Jebo te vrag!), red in the face, she turned her back and swept at the other end of the corridor.

The sound of children's crying was emerging from a couple of rooms. And farther down the corridor an old man was wailing, "Mama!" He was calling through the ages, from perhaps his ninetieth year to the middle of the previous century, for a time when he was a helpless toddler with a voluptuous mother, who by now was probably dust and bones in the ground in one of the rickety cemeteries in the hills. On his deathbed, and nobody attended to him. The cries stopped and there was a long moan, which trailed off and became a wet wheeze, assuming a ghostly echo from cavernous lungs.

Lyerka leaned her face against her father's arm, against the scratchy herringbone-patterned wool of his jacket. He put his hand on her head and petted her hair over her ear. "Daddy, can we just go home? It's better there."

"But you need help. They have good doctors here."

"What do good doctors do?"

"They make you healthy." Were they good? He wondered. They always behaved like they were; they boasted of their Zagreb Medical School education, which they said was the same thing as Viennese education, maybe even better because they adhered to the old standards of enforcing a huge repertoire of memorization.

He stood up and knocked on the off-white door, and as he knocked some of the cracked paint crumbled and fell on the floor.

"Comrade, not so violently! You're making a mess," said the cleaning woman. "I'll have to sweep again."

"Just you dare!"

He knocked again and then opened the door. A doctor was combing his hair in front of a mirror, and a nurse was putting lipstick on her wide mouth.

"Don't you see we're taking a break?"

"I see, but my child is terribly ill and we've been waiting. I never saw Comrade Vedric and his son come out."

"They didn't. They're in the other room. We've been working since six this morning. Fine, bring her in."

The nurse shook a thermometer, snapping her wrist thrice, and opened the child's mouth to put it in. Lyerka's teeth chattered. She bit the thermometer hard as her jaw clenched it.

"Oh my, don't bite through that glass," said the nurse.

After a minute, she pulled out the thermometer and held it up against the bald lightbulb. "It's forty-three degrees. That's way too high; she'll need a lot of aspirin and a cold press."

"Well, give it to her, then," said Nenad.

"Of course, we know what to do." The nurse got an aspirin, 500 mg, and put it on a spoon.

"Daddy, the puppy is hungry," Lyerka said. "Promise to feed him."

"Yes, I'll feed him, don't worry."

"Comrade," said the doctor, "who do you think will win in the semis, Dinamo or Hajduk? Tito is rooting for Hajduk, and so am I."

"I could care less. Just help her."

"I know. I need to keep some kind of conversation going to keep us sane, to keep you from worrying too much."

"Should I worry?"

"No, but we'll wait a little to see how she responds. Open your mouth!"

They put the spoon with aspirin on her tongue and then poured water from a glass into her mouth. The water spilled over. Lyerka coughed, and the aspirin flew out of her mouth like a little white dove out of a church window. The pill fell onto the checkered floor and rolled around, disappearing under the cupboard.

"Why are you spitting it out, darling?" asked the nurse.

"She can't help it," Nenad said. "It's a reflex."

"Let me see." The doctor shone a thin flashlight into Lyerka's throat, pressing down on her tongue with the handle of an aluminum spoon. "Hmm, her throat is too swollen and red; she won't be able to swallow such a large tablet. Fine, we'll crush the aspirin so she can drink it."

Lyerka gulped the water loudly and spat it out. "It's yucky!"

"You want more sugar, less sugar?"

"More."

The doctor read the sports pages. Nenad rolled the brim of his hat. After fifteen minutes they measured her temperature again.

"She's not responding yet. She'll need more time and a cold press and an IV and more aspirin. We'll have to keep her overnight, just like that boy."

"Should I stay here?"

"It's better if you go home and come back tomorrow morning. Nervous parents don't help; they make us nervous."

"Daddy, don't leave," Lyerka said.

"I'll be right back, and I'll bring you some ice cream."

She smiled and closed her eyes.

The ambulance drove the two fathers home. The boy's father, Vedric, pulled out a bottle of greenish slivovitz and swallowed two loud gulps. "My throat is too dry from all this anxiety," he explained. "Would you like a shot?"

"No, I don't drink."

"I don't know how you can stand to be sober in a situation like this. What is going on? Do you understand?"

"Who does?"

Nenad and Marta could not sleep that night.

"It's my fault," Marta said.

"What do you mean, your fault?"

"I was too happy and proud with how beautiful she was."

"What do you mean, was. Is. She is."

"I know, but what if she…"

"Don't say it."

The other two children slept.

"How about if we pray?" he suggested.

"It's that bad? I knew it."

"Prayer is a good idea either way."

He got out of bed and played the guitar, slowly, a church song.

"When will you pray, then?" Marta asked.

"God loves music more than our voices."

"How do you know that?"

"My soul knows that."

Early in the morning, before any redness showed in the paling sky, Nenad bicycled to the hospital. The little dynamo hummed against the tire and produced enough light to illuminate the unpredictable road ahead. There were a couple of hills too steep for the bicycle, and he walked up them and sweated despite the cold wind. Lonesome dogs were howling at one another from two remote hills.

He found a different doctor, who looked strikingly similar to the night shift doctor, except his hair was silvery; it looked as though the same doctor had aged a decade overnight, but it was definitely a different doctor, shorter and thinner, standing irresolutely with a couple of plump nurses in the emergency room.

"How is she doing?" Nenad asked.

"Who? We have lots of patients in the ward. There's some kind of epidemic."

"My daughter, Lyerka Vukov."

"Oh, yes, we can't get her fever down. It's still forty-three. And of course, with such a long fever, she's delirious."

"So, will she make it?"

"Let's hope so."

"Of course I hope. Can you do something more than hope?"

"I hope so."

"Are you joking or something?"

"We'll put her on IVs again so she doesn't dehydrate, and with more liquids in her body, she could cool down."

"Can I see her?"

She was red and her lips were green, and she mumbled about a puppy.

"Sweetie, I will get you the puppy. He's waiting for you."

Lyerka grasped his thumb, giving it a hot squeeze. But she had no strength to do it for more than a few seconds, and her hand dropped and she continued to moan. Her neck was swollen, bigger than before.

"What did she eat before she got sick?" asked the doctor. "Maybe she ate some poisonous mushrooms?"

"Not this time of the year—nothing's growing in the winter, other than oyster mushrooms, and those are never poisonous."

"Dry mushrooms? Old pork?"

"We don't eat pork."

"You are Jews? Adventists?"

"Neither, but we just don't. The problem is, she's had an inoculation against rubeola. What do you think is the problem?"

"I don't know, an allergic reaction. We'll give them some milk."

"Milk?"

"Yes, milk helps with allergies and poisons."

"She had plenty of milk. You have nothing stronger? No real medication against this?"

"We'll think about it. Just let me think."

"Well, think fast. If you save her, I'll give you ten thousand dinars."

Lyerka gasped and breathed fast like a dog after a long run. Her mouth was open, and her little red tongue trembled.

"And I'll sign over my forest to you," Nenad said.

"I'll do what I can."

The nurse placed wet towels over her body. They gave her an IV.

Nenad waited in the corridor, which was filthy with muddy print marks of boots of all sizes, in all directions. Clearly, people here walked in circles, disoriented and frantic as they waited, and so did he, with his hat brim rolled in his left hand and his right hand scratching a sore spot on his scalp, layered with dandruff, until it bled.

"The fever is going down, just a little, but it's in the right direction," said the doctor. "Don't panic. We'll do all we can, and we are talking to the specialists in Zagreb over the phone."

Nenad wondered whether the sudden activity by the doctor had anything to do with the offered money. The motives didn't matter; saving his chedo, his dear child, did. So the thing to do was to go home and raise the money. He bicycled back, first to Drago to ask him for a thousand dinars, which Drago gave him without comment. He rode home and collected his savings hidden in the attic under a pile of red roof tiles. He gathered ten thousand, a small fortune. With that he had planned to buy a new Opel or perhaps a Mercedes. So much for that. He bicycled back to the hospital. In a curve the bike slid over gravel, and he fell, banging his elbow like a child.

He took the same doctor aside, onto the muddied, spotted-marble floor of the dark corridor, near white-painted windows, and said, "Doctor, how is she doing?" He felt unsteady, and as he leaned against the window frame, thick cracked lead paint crumbled and peeled off in little sheets.

"To be frank, the fever has come back, and we can't knock it down."

"What is it?"

"It could be meningitis, as a side effect. Apparently there's a lot of it around."

"You call it a side effect? It sounds pretty major."

"Well, we don't know. We actually don't have the blood test results yet."

"What are you waiting for? I'm giving you ten thousand dinars—that's what a factory worker would make in two years—to save her. You have to try harder."

"It's not necessary. I'll do my best." But contrary to what he was saying, he stretched out his hand and took the blue envelope, with the stamp of the walls of Dubrovnik, and placed it in the right front pocket of his pants, keeping his hand in the pocket, deep, as though he was shifting his balls to a more comfortable position.

"You promise you'll watch her? Consult your best books and other doctors. Maybe there are American doctors in Belgrade at the embassy who would know about these side effects? Can you call them?"

"Yes, we'll call them. I'll do what I can. Let me go now—talking with you won't help her. We'll try a few things."

"May I go with you?"

"Better not at the moment. Just wait here, and we'll call you in."

Nenad paced up and down the corridor on the spotted black and yellow floor. The light of the thinly clouded day spread through white curtains and bounced off the floor in a jaundiced hue. What to think in a situation like this? He'd been under the gun several times in the war, and it felt simpler—immediate fear, possibility of a clean and violent end. He'd even had shrapnel lodge near his kidney, but two years after the war, it crawled out of him, and he woke up with a small wound bleeding calmly. The shrapnel looked like somebody's iron molar. He'd much rather 'be hit with shrapnel again. The mix of hope and fear only increased his dread.

He was not the only one pacing—there were four other parents. They all smoked. Nenad knelt near a bench and prayed. God, if you save my daughter, I will serve you and do whatever you want me to do. I will give biblical names to all my children. I will witness for you and go to jail if necessary. And if you don't save her, I will become a communist. Not that I am in a position to make threats, but isn't it a good idea to make friends in this godless country?

Before he could say amen, he heard a scream.

He stood up. A doctor was speaking softly to a mother and holding her shoulder.

"What, he is dead?"

"Yes, two children are dead."

"How about my child?" asked Nenad.

"Is Dara all right?" cried a woman next to him.

"Wait, not so fast. We'll give you the names."

"Is Lyerka alive?" Nenad hoped it would be another child, not his.

"Dara is dead," said the doctor. "Sorry to say."

"Are you sure? Maybe she just passed out."

"What can I tell you? This is a major tragedy."

"You couldn't do anything?"

"And Lyerka?"

"Alive, we are working on her."

Nenad kneeled against the wall and prayed on.

"Look at him, his child is alive, and he is praying to God," said a man. "And he has money. I'm sure he paid them."

"That's how it goes—the world always favors those with money."

"Maybe we should have prayed to God."

"He has probably given money to his God, too."

The two dead children were wheeled away, covered with white sheets; one had her eyes wide open, and the other had them closed, and on his eyelids were placed two sugar cubes to keep the eyes closed and to decrease the bitterness of death.

A few minutes later Nenad knocked on the door of the room with four beds. The doctor and the nurse were playing cards at a table. Next to them was a large red apple on an orange-colored plate.

"Is she alive?"

"Yes, she must be."

Nenad ran to the white bedside. Lyerka moved her face toward him and smiled. Her eyes gleamed; she looked radiant. Her hair emitted indigo-blue rays, or so it seemed to his wet eyes, refracting the light and intensifying it, as though he were sinking into the dark of an ocean and looking upward toward the glare of the unreachable sunshine. Nenad leaned over and kissed her forehead. It was astonishingly hot.

"Can't you give her more aspirin?"

"Oh, she's had plenty. She's running about forty-one. It's not all that bad. It used to be worse. It's going down, sort of."

"You think she will make it?"

"She might, she might."

"Is there nothing else you can do for her?"

"No, we just have to wait now, like you."

"And so you play cards?"

"And so we play cards. Health is a game of luck like cards. At this point we can only hope to be lucky."

He walked back to Lyerka. Her mouth was twisted, and her eyes were glazed. Foam floated down her cheek.

"Look at me!" he said.

But her eyes seemed to be looking beyond him, through the walls, into the clouds, reflecting the clouds, becoming gray. He had wasted her last minute of consciousness talking with the card-playing doctors. But maybe she hadn't been conscious in a while anyway.

"Don't you see, she's dying," he said. "Can't you do something?"

"Oh?"

Nenad looked into her eyes. They were hazing up, losing focus. A milkish hue covered the brown of her iris.

"We did what we could. Many children died from this inoculation. They gave us a dosage that was way too strong."

"Are you sure you did what you could? Maybe you gave up too soon? Isn't there some drug to keep the heart going?"

They didn't reply but looked for the pulse in her neck.

He couldn't look at the cloudiness in her eyes, and he put his large hand over her face and pulled the eyelids down. They sprang back up, halfway.

"Give me the apple," he said.

It was an old red apple from the late fall, with creased skin. He sliced it and put two moon-shaped slices over her eyelids to keep them closed. An apple was the first gift of God to man, so be it. Maybe the apple will help her see all the way back into paradise.

———

He held her in his arms. Her temperature was becoming normal. Why did she die? Maybe I didn't believe enough. But the whole world is full of unbelievers, and many of them do fine.

At home, when he brought her in, the older kids shrieked in fright. He laid her down on her bed. The siblings stood on the side and stared.

"Is she asleep?" Nada asked.

"You could put it that way," said Nenad.

Her mother turned ghastly pale and said, "I knew it."

"What do you mean, you knew it?"

"I'm not surprised. We were happy, we were too happy, for the first time in our lives, these last few weeks. And I was too proud. I boasted that evening how she could multiply. God has punished us. I shouldn't have bragged about what a beautiful child we had."

"Why do you think it has anything to do with you? Just now I thought it was my fault, that I didn't believe enough. Why do you think it has anything to do with us? Maybe God wanted her in his heavenly choir. Maybe she's happier there."

"She's not there. She's nowhere."

And now the funeral had to be arranged. There was no cash left in the house.

"Go ask them to give it back to you," Marta said.

"I can't ride to Pakrac now. It's too far away. I don't care, life is over. I'm exhausted."

"We must still bury her."

"I don't know what we must do. Maybe we can just keep her in the bedroom, maybe she'll wake up."

"Well, we must bury her; there's no other way."

"No, it's all over."

"Life goes on."

"It doesn't."

"It was so beautiful while it lasted. God gave, God took away."

"America took away."

Nenad bought a black flag on credit. Marta sewed it onto a pole, and Nenad stuck it out of the roof through a space between two loosened tiles. Sunshine streaked through one window, projecting a parallelogram onto the warped wooden floor.

He went to the printing press office in the center of the town, near the Hungarian Calvinist church. The press used to publish a weekly newspaper but now published only death notices and festival posters.

Darkness filled the house, unabated by the ceremony surrounding death. Rather than buy a coffin, Nenad built one and varnished it. Yes, she said he could build anything. How much nicer it would be if he were building a doghouse. Maybe if he'd let the dog come in, her happiness would have carried her through the poison.

Before going to bed, he went over to the table where Lyerka lay in state and kissed her cheeks, which were frightfully cold and rubbery. It was as though the real body had burned away and vanished into the clouds and what remained was a death mask made of some special mix of rubber, plastic, and bread dough. It seemed a peculiar chemical mix, such as only German and American technology were capable of producing. But that couldn't be—death and cold corpses existed even before. Yes, but this was an American death. Of course, my thoughts are all rubbish, futile spasms of strained nerves. Here she is, and the soul is still somewhere near her body or in her body. It couldn't have left so fast.

He drifted to sleep to the sound of two lonesome dogs howling at one another somewhere in the hills, and then woke with a start when a blinding light filled the room. But as he stood up the light diminished and lifted, flowing out the window. And he heard a voice: I have heard your prayers. Be patient.

"How can I be patient?"

There was no answer, and the light completely vanished. The night light—was it moonlight or starlight or ghost light?—receded into blackness.

"Who are you talking to?" asked Marta. "What is it about being patient?"

"God has asked me to be patient."

"Oh, Nenad, God doesn't talk to people."

"Yes, I saw him, his back. He passed through our room and nearly blinded me. I saw only the light after him, not his face, of course."

"What do you need to be patient about?"

"About Lyerka. We will see her again."

"Yes, when we die. You plan to die now?"

"You are cynical even now? No, God will resurrect her."

"Did God tell you that?"

"Not quite, but I am sure that's what he meant."

"How can you be sure?"

"Don't provoke me now!"

"I'm just asking a simple and reasonable question."

"No, you want me to doubt again. Doubt is what got me, us, into trouble."

He started to shout.

"Now, is that a way to behave at your child's wake?"

"You tell me. How is one supposed to behave? Is there a book of manners to explain that?"

———

Many people visited and wept at the sight of the blue child in the tiny coffin. Her rich black hair, curly and wavy, adorned her face. Schultz, the Baptist minister, came over and showed Nenad the article in the daily newspaper, *Vijesnik*. 81 CHILDREN DIE OF NEW VACCINE IN SLAVONIA.

"That's not that many. What, ten thousand got the vaccination, and my child had to die," Nenad said.

"Can we pray?"

"For her soul?"

"Yes."

"All children go to heaven," Nenad said. "They can't sin. Why pray?"

"We can pray for you and your wife."

"Don't worry about us, we'll do fine. It's too early for her to go to heaven. Let's pray for her resurrection."

"In a few minutes we will. But first I'd like to tell you something about the American system. There you can sue for medical errors. You should find out what company did this vaccination, and go to the American embassy and file a lawsuit. They do experiments like this in the countries without medical malpractice laws—in Africa, and here."

"You think they'd let me into the embassy?"

"You should ask for at least ten thousand dollars."

"Money won't bring her back to life. Money doesn't mean anything."

"You have other children. You could afford a better, healthier house."

"What, you are saying my house isn't good enough. It's filthy to you?"

"No, but it's a little dark and gloomy."

"The world is dark and gloomy. It's the vale of tears."

"So maybe it's not so terrible to think of your child now in heaven."

"Jesus resurrected children. He resurrected himself. He stayed dead for three days."

Marta came over and said, "Would you like some tea? Linden tea? It's good for the nerves."

"I'm going to my workshop," Nenad said.

There he cut poplar boards and framed a box with a little door and a slanted roof. The minister and Marta came and watched him, laboring in his cloud of reddish sawdust, but he didn't notice them.

"Who needs a doghouse?" Marta asked.

"You never know," Nenad answered. "It's good to be ready."

Later a procession was formed, and the casket was placed on a horse-drawn hearse. On its side, several wreaths hung, with black ribbon and purple writing expressing good wishes for Lyerka's afterlife. The parents and siblings followed immediately after the hearse, then uncles, aunts, and distant relatives, neighbors, acquaintances, and finally strangers, and lots of old women in black. The metal reinforcing the wooden wheels crunched the gravel in the streets. And on the side, not far from the coffin, limped a large orange dog with hanging ears and furrowed brows. He kept looking up at the coffin and whimpering quietly.

"Can you chase him away?" Marta said to Nenad.

"No, he belongs here. He's our dog now."

"We don't need a dog," she whispered.

"Yes, we do."

RASPUTIN'S AWAKENING

In Grisha's hungover state, the low sunshine of the mid-May morning glared and hurt his eyes. He cleared his throat and spat. His esophagus still burned as though on fire, and when he exhaled, smoke or steam came out of him. The night before, he had visited an old-style vodka tavern such as still existed only in Siberia (a wooden hut serving nothing but vodka) at the crossroads near Pokrovskoye, his village. He had spent all his money, and in the end gave up his sheepskin jacket, and his shirt, and his bronze necklace with a cross, and he would have given up his pants too, but the barman laughed and said, You'd have to pay someone to wear that! How did you mange to rip a hole like that? Your farts are that powerful?

No, I sat on a rock. And how about the boots? asked Grisha. They are made out of ox hide.

They look terrible and useless, too. They don't even seem to have soles—you dropped them somewhere?

I'll give you everything for one more glass of vodka, and you can give me your sackcloth so I wouldn't go home naked.

Sackcloth? What do you think, what era do you live in? Even an empty potato sack would be worth more than what you have. This is the end of your drinking for the night. One more glass and you'd have to crawl home.

Grisha had woken up in a ditch right outside of his two-story home. He had no recollection how he'd got there, whether he had walked or whether someone had dumped him. A red-eyed, perhaps blind goose had awoken him, mistaking his hair for grass and pecking at it. As he sat up, she hissed at him and he tried to kick her.

Grisha covered his eyes with his palms, massaged them, and looked after the flying goose. The sun flared up through tiny leaves of oaks, green and brilliant. The boughs spread out like huge arms, welcoming arms, looming in the light. They were thick black arms, with refracting light thinning them.

He passed by a large possession of a peasant. Geese were honking at him and sticking out their necks. There were tall hay-stacks, protected with wooden fences from deer and thieves. The wood wasn't just branches but narrow and hewn round laths. With these laths, one should make something much nicer. If he collected enough of them, he could make a sweat lodge.

He went home, hitched his old, emaciated black horse to a squealing cart, and collected a sharpened axe and a rusty saw. He rode back to the peasant's field, chopped and sawed the laths into the right size, and loaded them on the dusty cart.

The grass was turning green but was not tall yet. The soil was wet, and his boots got muddied. As he walked, they were sucked into the mud, and when he pulled them out, the mud sucked loudly after them, asking to swallow them again. The mud tried to eat his boots, displaying its bad manners, smacking its lips and slurping, but the boots pulled out, up, and then hovered before hitting the salivating mouth of toothless Mother Earth. The soil succeeded in taking off his left boot. Grisha stood like a stork, a gangly and yet sturdy stork, on one leg. The wet cloth wrapped around his foot unraveled and fell into the mud, revealing his large feet; his uncut nails curved and wrapped his large toes, thus giving them extra protection. Grisha swore, Fuck St. Catherine! He pulled out the boot, which was now filled with water, and emptied the water from it, and then slid his foot back in, as he continued to haul the beautiful wood from the fence to his cart.

The horse waited patiently on the road, dropping steamy dung now and then for entertainment. Grisha carried the wood. One plank gave him a splinter, and his hand bled.

Suddenly, the peasant came out from his house, running. He was clad all in brown and his face was brown too, weathered and creased. He had a long, broad nose with a horizontal crack in the middle. It seemed a sword must have hit him across the nose, cutting a wedge into it.

Grisha was tempted to run, but he looked into the peasant's eyes—they were pale blue like his. He seemed to be very similar to Grisha—perhaps a remote uncle? Maybe even his father?

You dirty ass, you're destroying my fences. You'll have to pay!

I am doing nothing of the sort. I will use the wood for better purposes. It's a sin to let such beautiful wood rot in the fields, and to keep God's creatures away from the grass.

I'll show you sin, you bastard. You come with me to the town court right away.

I am not going.

You better, said the peasant, and he grabbed one wood plank and held it in his hands.

What, you old *khui*, you are threatening me?

Yes, I'm threatening you, you *durak*!

Grisha swung his axe and it whistled in the air; he was not really intending to split the peasant's head, but to ward him off like a horsefly. And if he hit the peasant, he could finish the job that someone had started earlier—cutting through his head.

The peasant also swung and he connected—hit Grisha right between the eyes and over the nose. Grisha went down. Light flickered red in his eyes, warmth enveloped him. He felt very comfortable so bathed in light and blood.

He passed out, though a smile stayed on his face.

He came to as the peasant was feeling his neck, chest, and hands for signs of life. As Grisha opened his eyes, he felt a hard-on coming. It was cold, and he realized that in his fall his pants had slipped down.

You swine, I thought you were dead, said the peasant, both relieved and disgusted. You are a dog, just a dirty dog.

Grisha watched him in a beatitudinous state, in pain and pleasure.

He stood up. Above the brown hair of the peasant, who seemed to be a mirage arising out of the mud, he beheld a sight from before: the boughs spread like huge arms, welcoming arms, looming in the light. They were thick black arms, with refracting light thinning them. The arms of the tree appeared to him to be the arms of Jesus in disguise, resurrected Jesus, who was nailed onto a tree, having come from the trees, as a carpenter's son.

This was a call from God to go out and worship the wood, the nature that grows out of the ground, the resurrected soil.

From a distance, a bell tolled and the beautiful sound of metal buzzed over the valley. The vibrations of the air penetrated Grisha's ears and shook his loosened nose bones, so that his nose hurt even more. He snorted out blood, and his horse snorted on the road, in sympathy.

Grisha decided he would be a carpenter, like Jesus, and Jesus would live in him as long as he cut wood.

Why are you staring at me like that? You have brain damage? You damned thief!

You think that my collecting wood is stealing, but it is not stealing.

It's theft and destruction of property.

The whole land and all the wood belong to God. It's brazen of people to imagine that it is theirs. The people have stolen from God, and I aim to return the wood to God.

What people? You mean me? The peasant punched him on his left cheekbone.

Grisha saw lightning.

Why are you grinning, fucker! You falling asleep?

Oh, no, on the contrary. This has been an awakening for me.

You call that awakening? The peasant pointed downward. Pack it away, you dog. And wash it. That's my advice.

Spiritual awakening. I have seen the light.

All right. You'll get even more awakening at the magistrate's office. Let's go. Poshli!

Grisha knelt to the ground, crossed himself with two fingers, and said, Thank you, Lord.

Don't you have three fingers? asked the peasant. Don't pretend to be a believer, old or new.

Grisha stood up and said, I will follow you. I am a sinner and I am ready for justice.

Now you are willing?

Yes. And if you want, hit me again with that wood. You can punish me.

I could kill you and that wouldn't restore my fence.

Oh, you couldn't kill me. Please hit me again.

Why?

I deserve it.

I could, but it wouldn't do much good. At court, you will pay me back the damages, and you have to build me another fence. And maybe you can work for me as a swineherd.

Gladly. That's a wonderful job for a prodigal son.

You motherfucker, don't give yourself no fancy names now. You have nothing to do with religion.

You'd be surprised. I've just got a call from the Lord.

The peasant spat. At least you seem strong enough to do some work.

On the way to the courthouse, Grisha kept smiling and seeing visions of naked dancing angels. Most of them were female, and they had wonderfully loose breasts. Oh, thank you, Lord, he said. I thought angels were men.

What the fuck are you talking about? asked the peasant.

I am not talking to you, but to the Lord.

He looked at the trees above them, the boughs embracing the road ahead. He was a sinner, expiating for his sins in his own blood and the blood of Christ. He would be born again through this bloodbath and light; his old self would die, and the new one would be born. This was more complete than St. Paul's conversion on the way to Damascus, which didn't include baptism in blood.

He inhaled with delight the blood through his nose. It made strange slurping sounds. The peasant watched him with disgust.

My friend, you are a Godsend to me, said Grisha. You have no idea how beautiful this all is. May I kiss you?

The peasant pushed him and hit him on the nape with his fist.

Oh, thank you. I deserve this and more. I have been truly evil. Do you drink vodka?

Are you offering?

No. God doesn't want us to drink anymore. It is an evil drink.

How would you know? You look drunk to me.

I was, but Lord has sobered me up through your gracious fist. You know, I am not going to pollute the temple of the Holy Ghost, my body, by eating meat and drinking vodka.

The peasant kicked him in the ass and said, You call this temple?

I will eat only vegetables of the fields.

That's fine, but don't steal mine.

And moreover, fish.

He didn't remember that Jesus had eaten anything but figs, fish, and unleavened bread. Maybe he drank some red wine, but where would Grisha get red wine? The Siberian climate didn't welcome red grapes.

In order to dedicate himself to the matters of the spirit, he would need a wife, a sturdy one. He had admired the miller on the outskirts of the village who didn't need anything, other than the nails, from the Czardom. The rest he generated in his mill, and what he couldn't do, his powerful wife did. He boasted she was better and stronger than the mule—somewhat more intelligent and much more powerful. She could lift a mule, and she could till the ground and grow vegetables. And not only that: she bore him five children, and after each birth, she'd get up in ten minutes and go back to the field to till some more.

Now Grisha asked the peasant, Do you have any daughters? Perhaps I could marry one when I work as a laborer for you.

Yes, I have ten of them. You may not look at them. You touch one of them, I will nail your ass to a spruce—I'll fucking crucify you.

Grisha inhaled deeply, slurping. A drop of thick blood got caught in his windpipe and he coughed, and as he coughed his nose seemed to be splitting in sheer luminous pain.

CROSSBAR

On May 25, 2018, Dinamo Zagreb was trailing 1–2 against Crvena Zvezda Belgrade in a semifinal UEFA cup match in Maksimir, Zagreb.

Ten minutes before the end of regulation time, Milic, Zvezda's halfback, deflected the ball with his hand. The Dutch referee should have blown the whistle for a penalty, but he hadn't. Is it possible that he didn't see the hand play, and that the assistant referees hadn't either, while the whole stadium had? The fans were shrieking and throwing crackers, and for a few minutes the match was suspended. After a deliberation, the referees decided to let the game resume.

Big guys around me kept jumping, so that the cement stands shook. I have no idea how these guys grew up to be like bears—most of them in the range of six-two and six-six and weighing between 250 and 350 pounds. It struck me as unseemly that such huge guys would be so passionate about what short and stringy fellows did in the grass with a few balls. And yet I was one of those guys, jumping and shrieking. Ordinarily I was a civilized architect, with a taste for macchiato and single malts. At the beginning of the match, I was still a civilized human, but now, by the end, I had taken off my shirt and was hollering for blood.

The game became frenetic. See, I am cultured enough to use words like that (and I am even writing this whole thing in the damned English language, not all that patriotic of me) when I am away from the stadium—but in it, I am a Roman barbarian, wanting to see gladiators kick balls like chopped heads and heads like balls. Dinamo exerted fantastic pressure, shooting at the goal almost twice a minute, and then there was a great chance as Hodzic passed all the players, advancing to the goal. He was felled by Branislav Ivanović, who slid into his shins from behind. Ivanović is a fine player, Chelsea captain until recently, and I am sure he intended to get the ball rather than the player, but at that speed it's impossible to always be accurate. Anyhow, it was a clear penalty. This time, the stingy Dutch referee did whistle. Hodzic, the new phenomenal player for Dinamo, got the honor to shoot.

I knew Hodzic probably hated the Serbian players. Hodzic was born in 1992 in a Croatian village near Bugojno in Bosnia, and both of his parents were executed in front of him. He was raised by his grandmother as a refugee in Austria, and for him, eliminating Zvezda must have been a dream. He was a bony guy, with sharp cheekbones and a long hooked nose, hawk-like.

At the whistle, Hodzic ran, took a full swing at the ball, and the ball flew straight and hit the inside of the crossbar in the right corner. The metal resounded. The ball bounced onto the line and back up to the crossbar. The Zvezda goalie, instead of catching the ball, kicked it out and it landed on Hodzic's chest. Hodzic had another chance: he shot, and yet again hit the crossbar, and the ball flew far out, where Ivanović cleared it, sending it away into the Dinamo stands.

Now, you had to admire Hodzic's shots, even though they didn't go in. I think there should be a different scoring system, whereby each hit on the crossbar should count as half a point. Three crossbar hits would have amounted to 1.5 goals, and Dinamo would have made it. Anyway, the crowd was in a wounded state, throwing crackers. In the stinging smokescreen, anything could go, and it did. Many of us jumped over the fence, and right in front of me, I saw a man with a machete. Another grabbed the referee, a Dutchman by the august name Rembrandt, pushed him on the ground, on his knees, and the first one brought the machete down, beheading him. Somehow it looked normal at first...easy. The head fell and rolled and ended up sideways in the grass, stopped by the hooked nose.

I followed another group of hooligans, who got hold of Dinamo players, beating them systematically. Somebody knocked Hodzic down, and several people kicked him, shouting insults, *scumbag, good for nothing, they bribed you, didn't they, fucking whore...*

One of them said, I have a better idea, let's take him to the zoo.

I think I'd had a whole bottle of Hennessy during the game, and instead of sobering up upon seeing the beheading, I went along with the hooligans. Hell, I was one of them. I must admit, I even gave Hodzic a kick, somewhere in the kidney area, and I was one of the guys carrying him to the zoo. There were five of us, like pallbearers.

The zoo had modernized recently. It used to have barred cages, but now, with Croatia being members of the E.U., the zoo had to become more humane, and tigers got a bigger cage, an acre of land with trees to sharpen their claws, with a little pond to drink water from and bathe in, and these were new Siberian tigers, Putin's present to Croatia. Putin had just retired in Croatia, having bought the island of Ugljan.

Anyway, we tried to toss Hodzic over the fence into the cage, but the fence was too tall, and Hodzic fell out of our hands onto the pavement. He shrieked.

Oh shut up, you should have kicked that ball a little lower, we shouted. Why go that high with it, freaky ass.

Let's take him to the grizzlies, someone proposed. These august creatures were a political present too, from Obama, delivered by John Kerry, the foreign affairs minister, when he visited a couple of years ago. Croatia had proven to be a faithful peon of NATO, starting with smuggling arms for the Syrian rebels, sending peacekeepers into Egypt, etc.

There's a long tradition of presents in the form of animals. Indira Ghandi gave Tito elephants, Mao Zedong panda bears—so now we had grizzlies as well, named Bill and Hillary. Anyway, these guys were massive, male probably 800 pounds, female 450, even bigger than the Siberian tigers.

We had to climb the fence to throw him down, and he landed on the rocks, a little island. Bill and Hillary jumped to the island and sniffed Hodzic. We shouted, Tear him, eat him, but the bears merely sniffed him all over for a while and then licked his face. They did not bite him. Hodzic didn't move, sprawled and loose like a rag doll. Bill roared at us and jumped at us on the fence, but the fence was ten yards removed over a chasm, so he fell into it, climbed out, and growled at us, and jumped again. This time he managed to reach the fence and climbed it, and knocked down one guy and snapped his neck.

I ran. He bit my right calf and tore it right out. I pissed in terror and ran out of the zoo and into the streets, and a cab driver gave me a ride to the Rebro hospital. I bled richly and groaned until they cut off the circulation to my leg and gave me the shots to stop bleeding, and morphine. At first it had hurt less than I imagined it should—shock is a natural painkiller—and that's how I had managed to run for my life.

At the hospital, I passed out from loss of blood and the morphine. When I woke up, I was in horrifying pain. I stayed in the hospital for days. The surgeons patched me up, but without these muscles, it was clear I would limp for the rest of my life. At least I had the rest of my life. I wondered how Hodzic was doing.

Online, I found a report that Hodzic had a broken spine, a concussion, broken ribs, and a ruptured kidney. He was in critical condition at the Rebro hospital. Thank God we hadn't killed him. I swore I would never watch another soccer game, and I would never root again for any team. Croatia—both individual teams and the national team—was banned from international competition for four years anyway.

If I hadn't been there, the same thing would have happened; there were enough hooligans without me. Maybe I shouldn't feel terribly guilty, but of course I should.

When Hodzic recovered enough to go around in a wheelchair, I volunteered to take him places, and we became fast friends. I took him to Gradska Kavana every morning for a macchiato. Because of spinal cord damage, he'll never walk again unless medicine improves.

And what do we talk about? Anything but soccer.

For a whole year, I couldn't bring myself to tell him that I was one of the thugs, but one day, we were relaxing and in a particularly fabulous mood.

Let's go to the zoo, he suggested. I want to say hi to Bill and Hillary. You know, she saved my life by licking me and nursing me. I think I was clinically dead—I saw my dad and mom in Heaven, and we ate baklava together. I think there's life after death.

We took a cab. On the right side was the Dinamo stadium. He turned away from it.

I helped him get out of the cab with his electric stroller, and we went past the Siberian tigers to the bears. I had no reason to be glad to see them, but Hodzic shouted, Hello my friends! Both bears stood on their hind legs and made strange noises, something between a growl and a roar, but a couple of octaves higher, the way they would talk to a cub.

Beautiful, aren't they, he said. See, they remember me. Next time I am going to bring them some trout.

You aren't supposed to feed them.

I can do what I want. You'll help me get here?

Of course.

What would I do without you?

You know, Bill ate my right calf. I am not eager to feed him. I already did.

I know. I've read the articles.

You knew it all along? That's crazy. Why would you talk to me?

I saw the pictures, security camera pictures, and I could tell that one of the silhouettes was you. And then there were articles about the bear, how he killed two hooligans and tore up your leg.

And you don't blame me?

Of course I blame you, you ass, but I understand. You were a fucking hooligan. You weren't the ringleader anyway.

Generous interpretation.

Not generous. Let me show you something. He leaned over, opened his jacket, and I could see he carried an Uzi. Guess what that is for.

Security?

No. I am waiting for the other two. You are okay—you suffered, and I got to know you, and Bill avenged me, but when I see those motherfuckers, off they go.

Wow!

It's vow, not wow. So when can you come back to feed Bill and Hill with me?

As I stared at him, looking kind of like Stephen Hawking in his wheelchair, with thick glasses and a proper black jacket, with a red tie, I imagined I was seeing him for the last time. But am I stuck with him? If I quit seeing him, will he put me on the list of people to shoot? With thoughts like these, we couldn't be friends anymore.

Adios, my friend! I said, and turned my back to him, my hard-sole leather shoes crunching the sharp gravel, and a chill crept down my back, as though a bullet would go through me any second.

ACORNS

While the JFK Terminal 1 loudspeakers announced the last call for the nonstop to Frankfurt, John hugged his wife, Ana Tadic, burying his nose in her black hair. It smelled of her shampoo, chamomile and menthol.

"Are you really sure you want to go?" he said. "Dozens of journalists have been killed there."

"No interpreters, as far as I know."

His moustached lip slid past her mouth, brushing her cheek. Ana slid out of his embrace. "Don't forget tuna for Leo!"

She walked through the gate. Her steps thudded on the walkway. She sat next to a woman who was on her way to join her husband, a Baptist missionary, in Tirana.

"But most Albanians are Muslim," Ana said. "You want to convert them?"

"There are quite a few Christians among them. Are you trying to convert me to not converting people?"

"Touché."

Meanwhile, a curly-haired child insisted, "Read bookie!"

Ana envied the intimate joy emanating from the mother and child, and she resented herself for being such a poor sport. Now, at the age of forty-four, she wanted children. She and John had avoided procreation for a decade, as there were too many orphans in the world. Now she felt like an orphaned woman whenever she saw mothers.

One day later, Ana rode to Banja Luka, Bosnia, in a UN convoy. They ran into mudslides, passed houses smoldering in smoke, and checkpoints where they waited as the drivers and officers smoked with Serbian soldiers, giving them gasoline and cartons of cigarettes. *That's what a love of languages has got me!* she thought. In Cleveland, in the old ethnic neighborhood on the East Side, her father had taught her Croatian in the evenings when he wasn't too exhausted from factory work. He's died of lung cancer just around the time that Joe Eszterhas had moved from LA to Cleveland—with throat cancer from cigarette smoke—in a quest for healthy living.

Through a hazy dusk, Ana looked on as the mayor of Banja Luka and Colonel McGinnis toasted.

"What am I to translate?" she asked.

"Nothing for now," said the Colonel. "At least I know how to toast."

"Oh yes," the mayor said. "Tell him I'm inviting him to a local ballet performance."

Ana translated that while the mayor tiptoed, mincing his steps and wiggling his buttocks.

"Ah, that's all right," said the Colonel. "I'm not a great fan of the ballet."

"This is no ordinary ballet," said the mayor. "It's progressive, interactive. You get to meet the ballerinas, you participate."

Ana went along with them in a UN jeep.

The mayor said, "We won't need your help anymore. You stay out here and wait, until Petrushka is over."

Through crooked windowpanes, Ana caught glimpses of a dozen naked girls moving listlessly to quasi-folk Serbian music—Ceca, Arkan's wife, was singing—blared distorted through the loudspeakers. A woman fell down the stairs outside the building. Ana walked over to her.

"Don't touch me!" the woman said.

"Come on! I'm trying to help you."

The woman couldn't keep her balance, and her thin blue lips twitched. Ana wrapped her leather jacket around her, found out her name (Alma), and tried to keep her talking.

"They said it was a ballet performance," Ana said.

"You can see it for yourself what kind of ballet."

"Why did you join?"

"How can you ask?" Alma sighed, and then told her story.

In the spring, her husband was invited to a birthday party. He asked her, "Do you think I should go? I think I'm the only Muslim invited." She thought perhaps he should; maybe if he stayed friends with the Serbs nothing would happen to them. But he never came back from the party. When she went to the Serb's house to ask about him, the host invited her in for a cup of coffee. He acted surprised that her husband hadn't come back. He made a couple of phone calls, asking whether anybody had seen him, and then he offered her a meal of rabbit paprikash. After she'd eaten some, he asked her how she liked it, and she said it tasted great. She hadn't eaten in days. "Do you want to find out how I raise bunnies?" he asked. He opened a freezer with human body parts. She thought she recognized her husband's hand, but she didn't have much time to look. The man knocked her down from behind and, when she came to, the "host" was driving her to the bordello, which catered to the UN soldiers.

Ana managed to say, "We'll get you out of here. Just stay with me."

"Nobody can get me out of here." Alma pointed toward her belly.

The Colonel came back with a driver and a bodyguard; he combed his disarranged hair and said, "Let's go!"

They all climbed into an armored vehicle, accompanied by several camouflaged transport trucks.

"Who is this?" The Colonel pointed at Alma in the backseat.

"A rape camp captive," said Ana. "We've got to get her out of here."

"Oh, don't be melodramatic. Every hooker could make the same claim, of being a prisoner of bad fortune. She's all right here, she can make a living."

"Look at her! Let her go."

"Your job is to interpret, not to make judgments. Driver! Stop the car."

"If you throw her out," Ana said, "I'm quitting."

The Colonel ordered two soldiers to drag Alma back to the "dance club."

"In that case, give me a ride as well, to Split," Ana said.

"If you are that touchy, it's all for the best that you get the hell out of here." He chewed bubblegum, clicking his tongue. Ana glanced down his smoothly shaved, fleshy cheeks, purple with broken capillaries. The back of his neck was covered in curly gray hair. Thanks to his chewing, he resembled a partly shorn and fattened ruminating ram.

In Split, Ana waited for a couple of days in a hotel among many Bosnian exiles, who stared out the windows to the ships apparently sinking beneath the ever-so-slightly curving horizon.

Her neighbor on the flight from Split to Zurich was a pale woman in a black miniskirt. During takeoff, she whispered, "Bozhe pomozi!" Lord, have mercy!

Her name was Fata and her teeth were brown, some cracked. What a contrast—such delicate fine skin, big dark eyes, neat eyebrows, and then those terrible teeth.

"What takes you to Zurich?" Ana asked.

"The Devil himself."

When they ate, Ana noticed that the woman was missing her ring finger. Instead she had a red stub. The woman caught her noticing and said, "The chetniks couldn't get my wedding ring off because it was too tight. They took my husband to Omarska and said I wouldn't need the ring anymore."

Air turbulence made the plane suddenly sink, and the two women levitated above their seats for a second, kept from flying off by their seatbelts. Soon Ana dozed, but her ears popping woke her up again. Alma's teeth were chattering. She clutched Ana's hand. Ana wondered whether Alma was like a cat that, in cold weather, will curl up next to almost any strange creature, even a dog, for heat.

At the Zurich airport, she invited Alma to lunch, but Alma declined and took the escalator down to the train station in the basement of the airport. As she sank away from sight, Ana experienced sorrow and love for the afflicted young woman. Ana's dejection amounted to more than compassion; it was a sort of sickness at heart, and she recalled the Latin religious term that reminded her of that, *misericordia*; although it meant mercy, its roots were in the poverty and sickness of the heart. The beauty of the word made her shiver, as though she'd heard a stirring harmony of chords.

She walked to the ticket booth and bought airfare to Zagreb instead of New York. The brilliant Swiss organizers had arranged that the gate for the flight to Zagreb be right next to the one for Belgrade. Two groups of people eyed one another across the aisle malevolently and disappeared in the communal cigarette smoke, fed by both sides equally. While waiting, she called John in New York, waking him up.

"I'm so happy you've called! Are you safe?"

"Yes, I'm in Zurich."

"Your mission was so brief?"

"I quit the job in Bosnia."

"Really?"

"You told me to quit. But don't worry, I didn't quit because of what you told me but because of what I saw—how the UN works. The UN is a bunch of sex tourists and vultures. Now that I've had time to think about it, I must go back to gather evidence."

"You aren't coming home?"

Ana got a ride with a UN truck that was on its way to Omarska to deliver humanitarian aid to the local Serbs. From the town center, she walked to the outskirts, to the camp, a scattering of one-story barracks and storage spaces surrounded by barbed wire.

At the entrance a policeman in blue, with a red star on his cap, asked her where she was going, and she said she wanted to interview the camp director about the distribution of humanitarian aid. Looking at her lips and neck, he said, "I'm sure he'd love to talk with you."

Soon she was seated in the director's office, drinking muddy coffee. Through the windows she could see tall mountains in the distance, which were blue as well. She remembered that Leonardo da Vinci was the first to observe that all objects appear blue in the distance.

"Lijep pogled, zar ne?" *A beautiful view, isn't it?* She addressed him in Croatian, attempting to establish a casual tone, to ease the tension that made her knees tremble and her throat as dry as if she'd smoked pot, even though she hadn't done that since her college days.

"Yes, it's overwhelming," he said in an unusually high voice. "Often I just sit here and stare at the mountains. I wish I was a poet like our president, Karadžić, so I could put all this beauty into words." He smiled, with tears in his eyes. "So, you work for the UN?"

"As an interpreter."

"Oh, another writer."

"I said interpreter. But yes, possibly a writer as well."

"So I wasn't wrong. You know that all the leaders in this country are writers. Karadžić is a fabulous poet. Izetbegović is a lousy Muslim historian. Tudjman writes boring history books full of lies. Cosic, the president of Yugoslavia, was nominated for the Nobel prize several times, and if we didn't have this war he'd probably get it. Well, only Milosevic doesn't need to write. He has other ways of expressing himself. Oh, I admire writers. They have done so much good for this country. And you probably think I am a dumb peasant, don't you?"

"Why would I?"

"Don't lie to me, I can see it in your mouth, in your overly white teeth. But you know what? I studied history in Novi Sad." He waited to see what effect the statement would have on her and then asked, "Who are you going to write for?"

"The *Boston Globe,* I think. Possibly *Harper's.*"

"Herpes? We have no herpes here. Syphilis, yes, but herpes, that's an American thing. What do you want to write?"

"I simply want to find out how the prison functions."

He squeaked. "Sure, come with me. I'll show you how it functions."

He walked with her to a small windowless room. Anna hesitated at the threshold.

"What kind of journalist are you?"

Ana stepped into the dank room that smelled of salt, mold, and urine. She held her breath, and her heartbeat intensified.

"How come you speak Serbian so well?" he asked.

"Croatian. My roots are in this country. Somewhere around here."

"Let me see your press credentials."

"I don't carry those around. It's not prudent to have them. More than fifty journalists have been killed in this war already."

"Nice that you are so well informed. Are you a spy?"

"If I were, I'd have the press or diplomatic credentials— wouldn't come without a cover."

He grinned, revealing two large gaps among his upper teeth. "How much will you make if you get a sensational story? Give me thirty percent of what you make. Is that a deal? So what do you want? We can create news, whatever you want." He came closer to her and bent down to lean into her face, breathing out tobacco and decay. "We could arrange executions so you could witness and write about them and become famous. How about that? You'd just have to observe and write it all down, and you'd be bound to sell your articles to *Die Zeit*, *Le Monde*, everybody. In that case we'd do fifty-fifty."

Ana didn't know whether the man was earnest; for a couple of seconds she couldn't draw a breath.

"Are there any women captives?" she asked.

"You a feminist? No stories from me, then. You think I'm boring?"

"I'll take yours too."

The director walked her out of the cell and into another building. He called two guards in uniforms, coughed, spat, cleared his throat, and said, "Go ahead and interview her."

They led her into a large room with muddy windows and slammed the metal door shut. They pushed her into another room, where there were a dozen women, most of them asleep, some groaning, one singing slowly.

The guards ripped Ana's clothes off.

Ana kicked one of them. They subdued her, and as they pinned her to the floor, she said, "You can't do that. I'm an American."

"So?" said the first guard, with a sparse gray beard. "You've had lots of practice then."

"If something happens to me, American marines will attack your camp."

"Oh yeah?"

"That's how America works, protects her citizens."

The men laughed.

"I have AIDS," she said.

"You trying to protect us?" said the second, clean-shaven guard, who had a broken nose. "You hate us, and so you'd like us to get it if you had it. So you don't have it!"

"You'll rape others and spread it. I'm not trying to protect you but the other women."

"That's generous of you!" said the clean-shaven one. He raised his arm to hit her, but the bearded guard caught it and said, "Leave her alone."

"All right, you go first."

"She may be right. I don't want to mess with any strange diseases. Can't trust Americans. Plus this one's too skinny."

"Well, you have a point."

The two of them walked out.

Meanwhile, outside Bihac, an officer was talking to the plump and ruddy General Mladic. "Have you read the foreign papers? The whole world is in an uproar about Bosnian concentration camps."

"We have no camps. Education centers."

"And they talk about mass rapes."

"What mass rapes? There aren't nearly enough. Sometimes I worry…"

"Shouldn't we issue our troops warnings not to do it?"

"If you keep talking like this, I'll have to demote you."

"I'm not expressing my views. Just what the world reaction is."

"Don't you remember how when the Red Army was liberating Vojvodina, Djilas complained to Stalin that there were 110 reports of rape committed by the Soviet soldiers. Stalin replied, 'Here, our boys are dying on the battlefield and freezing to death, and you object to their having a little bit of fun?' Here, we are freeing Bosnia from the Muslim terrorists and you complain."

Mladic offered a full wineglass of plum brandy to the officer. They toasted the glasses, looking each other in the eye.

"Pretty good stuff, huh?" said Mladic. "By the way, when a lower officer was brought to be court-marshaled for rape, Stalin, who got hold of the case, promoted him to major. He knew that rape is good for morale. We have problems with morale. Go tell our boys to have fun."

The officer left. Mladic continued to lift weights, examining himself in the mirror.

Ana was transferred to a room with a few women. A bruised artificial blonde, Selma, told her the story of her abduction, straight from the mosque gate when she was going to pray. Another woman told her she'd been intimidated into leaving her apartment, and when she wouldn't several thugs came in, beat her and abused her. The women were not done with their stories when three guards came in and took them away.

In the morning, there was a performance. The camp director forced Ana to sit next to him. "I organized this just for you, so you'd have something to write about. Remember, fifty percent of income is mine!" Ana looked over her shoulder in fear and saw no policemen behind her, but she still didn't have the courage to leave.

Several officers sat in armchairs, drinking brandy and singing folk songs.

"You've read *The Bridge on the Drina* by Andrić, haven't you?" the director said. "Remember the scene where Turks impale a young Serb on a stick? Over the centuries, Turks did a lot of impaling, to humiliate us, and now we have to pay these Turks back."

"But these are no Turks," Ana said. "And even if they were, they wouldn't be the same Turks; all that was six hundred years ago, up to two hundred years ago, and who knows how much in fact..."

"You doubt history? In 1985, a gang of Albanians impaled a Serbian man on a broken wine bottle. The papers reported it all over the country, and the people went wild; this reopened the historical wounds of so much impaling by the Turks that the only way out of it is this, my friend. Here, we are balancing history! Watch now!"

He squeaked and majestically made a sweeping motion with his right arm. To Ana, he resembled an eagle in profile, with his beaky nose and slanted forehead, and just as an eagle has a feeble call, this predator had his squeak.

The policemen ordered a tall and bony boy to sodomize his silver-toothed father. When the son resisted, a guard cut off one of his ears with a rusty kitchen knife and forced him to go on. And then he shouted, "What? You can't get it up?"

"Come on," the squeaky cop said. "Let's be objective. If someone cut your ear off, you couldn't either. Enough of this. Bring in the next crew!" he shouted, and the bleeding son and the father were dragged away. Soon, guns reported and echoed their end.

"How do you like our little show?" the director asked Ana. "Not quite Broadway, but we could call it off-off-Broadway, right?"

Ana gagged in anguish.

"Would you like a typewriter?" he asked.

Later that evening, in a solitary cell, a guard put his knife to Ana's throat. "Undress!" he whispered loudly.

"Go ahead, cut my throat!"

"You don't mean that."

"Leave me alone."

And the guard moved away and sat on a bench, where he continued to drink from his half-full bottle of beer. "To be honest with you," he said, "I don't feel like doing it. But they'll kill me if I don't do it. They'll soon be here."

"Who'll be here?"

"The Major."

"Can't you pretend you've done it?"

"It wouldn't work. They would know."

"Who's they? What Major?"

The guard shattered the bottle. "Don't ask! What's that to you?" He approached her. "Don't resist. It'll be easier for both of us."

She withdrew, and he did not pursue her further. A big policeman walked in and settled down on the bench, lighting a filterless cigarette. "Why aren't you at it? Who taught you how to fuck? Your priest?"

"You make me self-conscious."

"Self-conscious! What opinion will Americans have of us if we don't do it?"

"You believe she's an American? She's obviously a Croat, no matter where she lives. Would you call a donkey, once you moved her to the Sahara, a camel?"

"Good point. So what are you hesitating about, then?"

When they attacked her, she passed out.

In the morning, the director walked into her cell. "How are we feeling?"

She didn't answer.

"I got a typewriter for you. You can come over and type in my office."

She went along in her tattered clothes.

"I'll get you some better clothes, too."

While she was seated at a desk staring at the white paper, the director talked to several Serb officers. "We have journalists up our asses. All kinds of international organizations want to examine the entire place. We've managed to keep them away from the back barracks. But at this rate, we'll get Boutros Boutros-Ghali... that journalist Gutman, Clinton, international lawyers, you never know."

"You're paranoid. Clinton is too busy with his orgies at the White House."

"In my place, you would be paranoid too. Look, even she's a journalist!" He pointed at Ana.

"Why do you let her write?"

"That's different. She's working for me. Anyway, you've got to truck all the bad cases away. Get me some healthy-looking ones, and we'll grease them up for a photo session. Twenty thousand DM. How's that?"

"Forget it. That's not much. Shoot everybody who doesn't look good and bury them in the woods."

"I don't want any freshly turned soil around," the director said.

"All right, a couple of truckloads without traces. That will be fifty thousand."

A truck was leaving through the rear gate of the complex, transporting women prisoners out, up a steep road. The tormented people collided with one another in the dark as the truck clanked over rocky gravel and slid along sharp curves.

When a guard bowed down to light his cigarette, Ana jumped out of the truck. She rolled on the road, scraping her knees and elbows. The guard shot after her, but the truck kept going. She walked gingerly through the heavily mined woods. At dusk, she heard wolves howling in the distance. A hundred yards away, an explosion. A boar stepped on a mine. Ana found its foot, still warm, its scorched flesh smoking.

Later she tried to sleep on a heap of windblown leaves. Her teeth chattered from the cold. Nearby a nightingale whistled her melody to the rhythm of a woodpecker that would peck slowly, only to accelerate into bursts of hollow wood-drumming. All the other sounds vanished; the two birds quieted the forest, enchanting it. Amidst those liquid sounds floating and echoing, she fell asleep.

In the early morning, she ate acorns and wild onions, which didn't do much to assuage her hunger. She stepped on a copperhead. The snake lashed at her, trying to bite through her jeans. Ana ran, and the snake jerkily darted after her for several yards, spitting out its tongue, and then vanished below a fallen tree. Vultures circled at an angle from her. She avoided the spot below them, afraid of what she might see there.

From a distance, she heard the bleating of sheep and the laughter of men, echoing together from two hills at either side. It had the strange effect of the past and the present creating the same cacophony.

Several men were beating a young man. They stripped him naked, tied him to a spindle well, and stuck a beanpole up his anus.

"Turk, how do you like the Greek way?"

The man passed out. Blood flowed from his nose.

The men slaughtered a sheep. They put a stake through it and grilled it. They drank. They reminisced about what happened the first time they got drunk, as kids. A grandfather taught one of them, at the age of ten, to drink slivovitz. Another one was self-taught, discovering white wine in the pantry when he was nine. A third one was given cooking wine one harsh winter at the age of eight. It seemed incongruous to Ana that these men would have childhood memories. At one time, they must have been charming little toddlers. The men withdrew into the house.

Ana quietly approached the young man and untied him. She whispered to him that they would run away together. He crawled and she helped him.

Soon afterward the men came out and looked in a small circle around the house, shot randomly into the bushes, and tore more flesh from the sheep, gnawing at the bones.

The young man's name was Hasan. At night, they slept together for heat. They hid away from any potentially human sound. They ate mushrooms they found; in a mix of ceps there were some bitter boletes. Hasan claimed they were medicinal and perked up after eating them.

Explosions resounded in the distance. There seemed to be an artillery exchange from two nearby hills.

"There must be two armies," said Ana.

"There could be three."

"Yes, but which one is the right one for us?"

"The side that shoots less would be the Muslim or Croat side. Serbs have heavier guns and more ammunition."

Indeed, from one hill there was a constant barrage of artillery, and the explosions resulting from it were louder, while from the other side came only sporadic fire.

Hasan and Ana crawled up the quieter hill. When they were close to the top, several bullets hit rocks next to them and sent rock shards and dusty smoke flying around them. Hasan shouted, "We are your friends!" With their arms up they walked to an entrenched Muslim regiment. While they were being interrogated as to their identities, Ana saw John in a green Muslim uniform. John shouted, "She's all right, she's my wife."

"My God, you!" she cried. "What a coincidence!"

"Not quite," he said. They hugged.

An explosion nearby interrupted them, and they all crouched in a trench.

"What are you doing here?" she asked.

"After I couldn't find you, and I looked all over, I thought I could go to the front and write real war journalism. Hardly anybody writes from the front. And these guys here said, All right, if you want firsthand experience, here's a gun."

As the battle raged on, Ana ignored everything—including John and the nearby shelling—to write down her observations from Omarska. Several hours later, she gave them to a courier, who was on the way to Jajce anyhow, with the instructions to photocopy and mail the pages to several addresses, which she wrote down from memory.

Ana and John stayed with the Muslim regiment, defending the hill, for two months. For the most part, there was just a lot of squatting, cleaning, card playing, boredom. Rain drizzled almost constantly, and staying warm wasn't easy since they couldn't light fires. A contingent of radical Muslims prayed frequently, kneeling eastward outside of the trenches, ignoring danger, and among them were Afghani and Iranian volunteers with thick beards and glistening eyes. There was a division between the secular and the religious soldiers; the religious ones stayed away from the side where there were women, they did not look at them, and so sex under these circumstances could not be easy. Nevertheless, at night John made erotic overtures, and Ana rebuffed him.

"What do you want me to do? You want me to look elsewhere?"

"Go ahead."

The thought of sex, any sex, made her shudder. And she had so many thoughts she couldn't communicate with John that she felt more intimacy being by herself than talking with him.

John stroked her cheek. She didn't have memories of her rapists at that moment, but she flinched nevertheless. And then she worried about how he must feel, and in a moment of compassion she stroked him back, but when he touched her breast she said, "No, not yet."

"When, then?" he asked.

Suddenly there was a commotion outside the trench, branches cracking, the stamping of feet, huffing. In the moonlight, silhouetted human figures rushed at them. The Muslims fired, and Ana fired her semi-automatic. The men kept coming and falling before reaching the trench, until none remained. Some of them were gasping and groaning, praying and swearing. The Muslim soldiers kept shooting at the sounds, and after a while, the moans of agony ceased.

In the morning, the Muslim soldiers examined the several dozen dead. Most of them were Russian volunteers, still smelling of booze even in death. The Muslims took the rifles and gold watches, which must have been stolen, and examined their papers. Ana stared at the corpses with a certain degree of horror. But within the horror, she could discern a sensation she was not proud of, but which was there, of satisfied rage. This was some kind of revenge—unfortunately not on those who had injured her, but still on members of the same army. She was sure she had killed at least three men. And she could have kept shooting, even after the attackers had fallen, at their expiring sounds.

Most of the soldiers dug into the ground with shovels, struggling through oak roots and rocks to bury the dead. Two large graves weren't quite enough to accommodate all the bodies and, tired of digging in the rain, the soldiers carried the remaining bodies away and dumped them down the ridge into a ravine, where wild animals, crows, and vultures would dispose of their remains.

All that day Ana couldn't eat, under a spell of adrenaline, and her heart beat strangely, in rushes and slowdowns. She felt like vomiting, which she attributed to the disgust and horror of being among so many dead. However, the following morning she had acute nausea, when she was thoroughly exhausted and sleepy. She asked the company nurse whether she had a pregnancy test kit.

"Yes, of course, I always carry them. We run into so many rape victims."

The result was positive, a thin purple line.

What she had once hoped for, and later feared she could not have, was now growing inside her. Her mood alternated from absolute dejection to elation, and she didn't know what should be a reasonable response.

Ana told John she was pregnant.

"When did we have sex last? Four months ago? And you found out only now?"

"Well, yes, I don't think you're the father."

"Here I thought you were saving the world, and you go screwing around!"

"What do you think? I was raped by two guards in the camp."

"Why didn't you tell me?"

"I am telling you. I've seen so much suffering that I didn't want the pity for myself. Or shame. In a way, I felt proud that I had taken up the suffering so directly upon myself. Forget sympathy. Suffering the same pain the women I talked with had suffered, and writing about the horrors firsthand, well, that seemed the right way to me. Except I still didn't want anybody near me to know. Not that I had planned it that way. Still, I didn't want unpleasant conversations after. But now, go ahead."

"Get an abortion. No reason to have a reminder for the rest of your life of what happened!"

"At least the child had no decision in that."

"I don't think you have any choice, really."

"You want me to abort here? You want me to risk my life?"

At night, however, Ana couldn't sleep, and the nausea grew worse, but she couldn't tell whether it was from angst or only from pregnancy. Flashes of the rape, the faces of the potential fathers woke her up, and she thought, I should get an abortion.

After the onslaught of Russian volunteers, the Muslims shifted their position, attempting to circle behind the mountain held by Serbs. They left only twenty soldiers behind to keep shooting, so their manoeuvring wouldn't be obvious.

On the way through a village, Ana saw little children playing basketball with a teddy bear. Clearly, they didn't have a ball, but the teddy bear flew around amidst children's happy hollering. Ana was elated at the sight of children, their little hands and fingers, tiny mouths, big eyes; was it their lack of self-consciousness or innocence or freshness that was attractive? And she knew there were children playing like that on all sides, Serbs, Croats, Muslims, Albanians, from all sorts of parents, and this knowledge helped her decide right then that she would not abort, because a child, no matter out of what circumstances, is always innocent. Adults, that was a different matter. Hadn't even she become a murderer, hadn't even she experienced a glimmer of twisted joy in murder? Twisted by desire for revenge or survival, but twisted nevertheless. Yes, adults could be corrupted, and often were, adrift in a chaos of revenge and hate. But children? After all this, she had no more doubts.

Ana and John stayed in the army for one more month. He could not forgive her deciding against an abortion. The more time passed and the less time there was for an abortion, the harder his features grew and the easier she found it to keep drifting away from him. He still tried to persuade her. "Get an abortion. You'll always have to think, my child was born as an act of violence. Not love. A child of hate. Horrible."

"Yes. Horrible. But it would be wrong to think about it that way. The men doing it—it's nothing genetic. It's the culture, the strategy, the mass rapes, and it's possible that they were forced to do it. The same men could have under different circumstances become wonderful citizens, kind, generous....true, they became monsters, but they could have become saints."

"You really believe that?"

"And you really don't?"

"I...I believe in the bad egg theory. Anyway, this means you can have a kid. We'll keep trying, and it's going to work. But now..."

During the march around the mountain, she watched the foliage of red oaks glistening in the sunshine. Everywhere, the rusty color was seemingly bursting into dark blue-tinged flames from the distant mountains. While gazing out, she slipped from the muddy path and fell at least ten feet before hitting the ground and cutting herself on a rock. Her shirt and skin over the abdomen had torn, and she bled.

John got a bottle of plum brandy to celebrate. "High time! The rock did the job, I'm sure, but do speed it along, darling. Drink half of this!"

"I don't see what you're rejoicing for," she said, and looked at him with momentary hatred.

"It's either me or the rape child," he said.

"In that case, we've decided."

"The rock has decided. And don't worry. We could have another child."

"I don't want another child. I want this one. It's not even a matter of just having a child for the sake of having a child. I want this one."

The nurse didn't know what her chances for keeping the child were. To get medical attention, Ana walked with several locals who knew a way around Bihac into a sliver of Croatian territory. Although exhausted, Ana stopped bleeding during the long march, and the pregnancy held. The following day, she felt strong, her body in equilibrium such as she had never experienced before. John, who could no longer communicate with her, left. Ana didn't ask him where he would go, as that was now irrelevant to her.

In Zagreb, on a tram, people read reports about mass rapes in Bosnia in *Vecernji list* and other dailies. Ana fleetingly wondered whether her report had contributed to the stories coming out into the open worldwide, but she was preoccupied more with observing the women right there. Many women stared at the floor, and among them was Selma, the blonde from Omarska. Her eyes were vacant; she seemed to be out of her mind. She was singing Serb folk songs loudly, out of key. Ana recognized her, called to her, but Selma did not respond. Some people shouted at Selma and beat her with folded newspapers—the very newspapers that reported on the rapes of which she was an extreme example—but she paid them no mind and continued singing the songs she had grown up with. Ana wondered whether she herself appeared like that to John, out of mind, out of key. But she could not think of a song to sing. When she stepped off the tram, she breathed in the cold air, glad that she felt no pain in her abdomen.

In front of a woman's clinic, dozens of scarfed and pregnant women timidly came to a large gate that had gray lead paint peeling like snakeskin. As Ana walked past them, she marveled that there was a life in her life. How could she want to harm it? She walked to the corner grocery store to feed the life within her with dark bread and walnuts.

WHEN THE SAINTS COME

Davor had been wheezing for days, and he gasped in his sleep and talked about Armageddon, global warming, and the vanished Boeing 777. Even awake, he talked about the 777 as the ascension airplane—all the people onboard went straight to heaven, and the rest remained on the ground, awaiting the wrath of God.

"You're not right in your head," his wife Alana said. "Since when have you been religious?"

"I used to be very pious as a kid, until I discovered girls. The way I understood it from my minister, it was either girls or God. I chose girls."

"Seriously, your breathing is terrible. You should give up smoking and go see a doctor."

"I've given up booze. That's good enough. You can't expect me to give up everything fun."

"This doesn't look like fun. Just look at you—you inhale and spit, and make faces like your tongue is burning."

"It is burning and it's not fun. I don't even get a kick from it, but I must do it. Some kind of devil has possessed me, and he's stronger than me."

"I think you've developed asthma and chronic bronchitis. Do your lungs hurt?"

"Can they hurt? Major organs don't."

"You have to take care of yourself!"

"But why? I've lived longer than my father, who died at the age of fifty. I thought that was my deadline. I've had ten extra years. Actually I used to think I would die even earlier than that, because I believed in the biblical verse, *Obey your father and mother lest your days on earth be shortened.*"

"Is there such a verse?"

"I was an evil kid. I fought a lot in a street gang, stole, drank. I have no explanation why I was drawn to bad things, other than that it was some kind of freedom or that I was possessed. No matter what, I thought I would die young, maybe ten years younger than my father. That I've outlived him is obscene." Davor blew out smoke and felt like passing out. "Can you fix me some Turkish coffee?"

"I will, and then we'll drive to Rebro Hospital in Zagreb."

The following day, after X-rays and blood tests, Davor faced a bald pulmonologist.

"Gospodine," the doctor said. "This is the worst part of my job." He cleared his bumpy throat.

"Obviously you have bad news. Go on."

"You have lung cancer."

"Oh. Is it a death sentence?"

The doctor remained silent for a few seconds, scratching his bald head, which had a wine splash of a birthmark that looked like Sicily. He leaned forward and peered into Davor's eyes. "No, medicine has advanced. We have many ways of treating lung cancers, and almost half the people survive it. It also depends on how advanced it is and what kind of cancer it is."

"Well, you said it was lung cancer. I thought there was only one kind."

"That's what we used to think, but there are many kinds, as many as there are varieties of snow in Alaska."

"How advanced is it?"

"You'll find out when we transfer you to the cancer ward for further tests."

And he found out that it was stage three, pretty late. He was content, nearly happy—he owed it to his father to die young. He'd lived too long already. And what more could he expect of life? Yugoslavia was gone. His older son lived in Belgrade and never returned his calls, and the younger one had died of a drug overdose in Stockholm, where he went as a guest worker. True, he had a fine wife in Alana, but even that had become a drag. She expected too much lovemaking and he found it too much work. He ran out of breath quickly and his body lost interest. Now he knew why—he didn't have the lungs for it.

His doctor and wife told him he had a chance of recovery only if he quit smoking and did his best to be healthy, and he listened, although living might be more work than not living. He daydreamed about how relaxing it would be to be stone dead.

He saw his old friends and forgave everybody all the debts they owed him, demonstratively. He went to Baptist church services on Sundays and Thursdays. He would go in peace.

He enjoyed each breath he drew, each sighting of red squirrels flying from branch to branch, and he relished drinking warm spring water in the center of the park, because he knew each of these little events could be unique, and the last of their kind.

Stage three small-cell cancer, survival rate fifteen percent, based on old statistics. I am done for, he thought, and strolled to his father's grave, and said, "Dad, I will see you soon. Are you glad?" Sunshine sifted through evergreen needles and flickered off the black marble stone, winking, and he wondered how it was possible that such a bright light came off a black stone.

At night he used an inhaler with cortisone. When he didn't use it, he gasped. And when he was falling asleep he was not sure whether he was passing out, falling asleep, or dying. He dreamt of French airplanes crashing in his backyard, snakes in his basement and in the living room, and floods coming up to the window on the second floor, carrying the empty coffins of his mother, father, and younger sister. A fourth coffin filled up with water, about to go under, and it contained his own yellow figure.

In the morning, it took him a while to come to his senses. His wife brought him Turkish coffee in bed, and he drank it plain, bitter, without sugar, as Alana had read that sugar was carcinogenic. Alana studied the writings of David Servan-Schreiber online, curious how to vanquish cancer with healthy foods and spirituality. The French scientist had just recently died of brain cancer after a fifteen-year struggle with it. Davor ate mostly vegetables and fruits and drank green tea. On the sly he put some sugar into green tea, which otherwise tasted like rotten hay. Hibiscus or red zinger he enjoyed plain.

"At least you are not tempted to drink slivovitz," Alana said.

"I'm amazed that you managed to quit smoking with me," he said.

"After you were diagnosed, how could I smoke? I don't miss it at all."

"It might be good to get some marijuana."

"You aren't allowed to smoke anything."

"There's no proof that smoking caused my lung cancer. Maybe years of burning wood in this Dutch stove did it, maybe the war, all those bombs, who knows, maybe they had depleted uranium. Smoking cigarettes—that could be American propaganda. Maybe I am dying from American propaganda."

Birds chirped outside the windows, swallows and finches. It was early spring in Lipik. Davor hadn't been into flowers before, yet now he saw the world differently and loved the forest flowers whose names he didn't know, some white, like little bells, others blue, yellow, purple. After a dreary, colorless winter, the ground had burst in the full spectrum of a rainbow, as though it had become the heavens, and who's to say it hadn't, as our earth is part of the celestial harmony, God's design. Now that he was sure he was dying, parting from a dreary life, Davor began to feel not only tranquil, but also happy—so happy that he began to fear that he would lose these moments of beauty, that he could not hold on to them, and thus the fear of losing the glimpses of beauty transformed into a fear of death just when he thought he was completely beyond it. The certainty of death enhanced the colors of life, and the colors made Davor feel more alive than ever, and swelled within him a desire to live.

And he thought, fifteen percent survival rate. Why, I will be in the fifteen percent. I will walk, pray, love. Maybe I will live to be ninety, who's to say I won't? And fifteen percent is an old statistic; maybe new treatments increase the chances. Maybe I'll live on carrots and walnuts, like a rodent.

But then chemo and radiation therapy came along, a dark phase of hair loss, feebleness, pain, and incessant nausea. His wife was always there, at his side, steady, patient. Alana was his second wife. The first one left him when he was still an alcoholic as a *Gastarbeiter* in Stuttgart. Although Alana was twenty years younger than him, she stuck by him. He'd heard rumors that she'd had lovers before him, perhaps even during their marriage, and he was jealous, but he repressed his jealousy. She certainly met a lot of people as a newsstand saleswoman. In this town and country, where half of the people were unemployed, it was a great thing to have a job. He couldn't mind that. On his own, as a car mechanic, he probably couldn't make enough for the basic bills. Twenty years ago, when the war had ended in Croatia, it was a good trade—there were many old cars in need of fixing that worked on pure mechanical principles. But now, even though people couldn't afford new cars, everybody had them somehow, and since cars were completely computerized, and Davor thought he was too old to learn new tricks, he was getting less and less work from more and more marginal people to work on progressively less and less worthwhile cars, for less and less. Cars that used to cost 20,000 Deutsche marks were now worth 1,000 euros. Changing a clutch in a car worth 10,000 euros, he could charge 400 euros. But now that the whole car was worth only 1,000, nobody wanted to pay forty percent of the car value for a peripheral part—they'd rather ditch the car up the hill outside of town for raw iron. The going rate was 100 euros for a plateless piece of junk. In other words, half the car value would be poured into a part, and if you added new tires, brakes, you'd spend the whole amount.

Even before his diagnosis of lung cancer, Davor had become completely dependent on his wife's income. His was good enough for cigarettes, coffee, and electricity. On the other hand, he lived in the solid walls of his patrimony, a three-story redbrick house his father had built with his own hands. It was a redbrick because he'd died before he could stucco it, and Davor had other priorities when he took over. It looked good in red, he claimed. So, no, he was not exploiting his wife, as she had free rent in his palace, his father's palace. It was all fair. But her working in public, to return to the first point, made him jealous. Sometimes she exposed her cleavage a little too much. She did it for him, and then when it wasn't him, it was all still there for the whole town; whoever wanted to buy *Jutarnji list* (Morgenblatt) could take a peek at Alana's sloping breasts and shaded thighs. If he'd been drinking, the way he used to in Stuttgart (oh, die Bier-gaerten!), he would have probably come out and complained and perhaps used a heavy hand in the Balkan tradition. Sometimes he listened to the Meho Puzic folk song, "Majko, il me zeni il mi gitaru kupi." *Oh Mother, either find me a wife or a guitar, because a man must hit on something.* His father had, in moments of inspiration or desperation, beat his mother. Not often, maybe once a year, maybe less, maybe it had happened three times in his childhood, but it left him and his siblings terrified for good, and strangely it imprinted that pattern of marriage in his mind. He was a cordial and soulful man who, now and then, when drunk, was a heartless and soulless man who beat the hell out of his first wife, thrice, and so she left him to marry someone in Belgrade who would continue this horrifying Balkan tradition until she divorced him too. The younger generations suppos-edly didn't do it anymore, but then, they indulged in soccer hooliganism and war.

He took the chemo better than expected and suddenly he had more energy than he'd had in years. He had no desire for ciga-rettes and wondered why he had ever bothered. But that meant he couldn't go out to cafés and bars. In most of Croatia, the smoking ban in eating and drinking establishments had been lifted. The country had reverted to the Yugoslav days, becom-ing one huge stinging tobacco cloud. He bumped into people in the streets and was more sociable than he'd been in decades. *Memento mori* had improved his life tremendously and kept him out of bars. He feared the oil and gasoline exhausts in his shop and in the streets.

"If it's God's will, I will gladly go," he thought.

In the local travel agencies, he saw a sign: seven-day excursion to Jerusalem, 500 euros. Four-star hotel, guided tours, everything included in the price. Alana encouraged him to go. "If we go," he said, "there'll be that much less you'll inherit from me."

"Don't worry about that. All the money you have will be spent on your funeral expenses," she said. "It's cheaper if you live than if you die."

"I've seen budget cremation advertised, basically the same price as the trip for two to the Holy Land. It's a trip for one to Hell."

"No matter what, you take a trip to the Holy Land. But why not try Jerusalem first. I'd like to see it too."

"But you're an atheist."

"I was raised a Catholic."

"How many times have you been to church in your life?"

"I think five. Three Christmases and two Easters. Six. Once for Baptism. Missed Confirmation."

They landed in Tel Aviv on Purim and spent a night there. The city was a carnival, a Rio—people in masks, dancing, singing. The following day in Jerusalem, Purim continued with people dressed in costumes, wearing masks. But the day after that, cleaning crews collected the remaining debris all over the city.

Alana and Davor didn't want to be with the tourist group, so they walked into the Old City to see the tomb of Jesus and the Western Wall on their own.

"This dry air feels fantastic," he said. "Sun and dry air, a great combination."

They entered through the Damascus gate, descending the stairs past oranges and olives and nuts and sneakers and sunglasses stands. The call to prayer blasted at them from all sides over cranky loudspeakers.

"In ancient days, they couldn't do it this loud," Davor said. "They probably complain about technology, and then use it to complain about it. But what do I know?"

Walking down Via Dolorosa, Davor was dizzy from all the spices, the sun, the heat. They climbed on huge foot-polished cobbles behind wailing pilgrims from the Philippines. Near the entrance to the Church of the Holy Sepulcher, three soldiers in light green fatigues laughed, swaying submachine guns under their arms. Davor and Alana entered the gate and faced the smooth pink-red rock on which the body of Christ had been laid out once he had been torn off the cross. Amazing, thought Davor. He knelt down, as several other people did, and kissed the rock. Thousands of people had kissed the pink marble, why wouldn't I, he thought. Well, maybe that's why—all their bacteria frolic on the rock.

"Can you imagine?" Davor said. "His body was right here, on this rock."

"Yes, I'm visualizing it. Was he still bleeding?"

Deeper in the cathedral, they joined a line coiling around a small ornate chapel. The cathedral contained a chapel, like a Russian doll, which contained the tomb where Jesus resided for three days and three nights.

"Hm, so much gold," Davor said. "I wonder what it was like without all the gold before."

"Yes, you kind of have to subtract the cathedral, the chapel, the precious metals, and then see the rock for what it is."

They climbed the Golgotha, just to the right of the entrance to the cathedral, inside it, elevated some eight meters.

"All so close?" Davor commented. "I thought they were farther apart, so you'd have to walk a little. And I thought it was a higher hill. But amazing. The crosses are here. I read that the cross of Jesus is the real cross. Empress St. Helena found it down the hill from here. Some durable wood!"

"The dry air does it."

"But it's moist underground in the cave where she found it. Maybe God protected the wood so it wouldn't rot."

They went down the Golgotha, and beneath it, in stone, was the grave of Adam.

"Look, the walls are red," Alana said.

They overheard a group of German tourists. The tour guide, with a heavy Yiddish accent, said, *"Das ist das Blut Jesus Christi."*

"That's the blood of Jesus, you heard that?" Alana said.

"Well, how could it still be here two thousand years later?"

"Why not? If you believe in the resurrection, which is a bigger miracle, why not believe that this is the blood of Christ? It's the erythrocytes from the blood of Jesus, containing red iron."

"It does look impressive," Davor said.

A group of Coptic monks in brown robes and beards of varying strengths and thicknesses sang in the cave of St. Helen, which being some hundred feet underground was pleasantly cool. They chanted and danced, celebrating the cross. Davor imagined how delightful it must have been for the empress to find the cross and to coat it all in gold and preserve it. But wasn't the church burnt down to the ground? Did the original cross burn as well? Or maybe the wood was fireproof? Was it cedar?

Next they went to the Mount of Olives and the Gethsemane garden, and read about the temptations of Christ. Davor knelt in the church, where Christ must have knelt, and repeated his words, "God, if it be thy will…"

Alana wept as she listened to him. "You know what, I believe in Christ now and in God. This makes so much sense to me. And that you're suffering like that—that is already saving my soul. All we are is soul."

The following day, they passed through the security and walked to the Western Wall. He wore a baseball cap, and that was good enough not to have to rent a yamaka, and she rented a shawl to go to the women's side of the wall, about one-third of the full length of the wall. Davor came to the wall, nearly blinded by the intense sunlight, and prayed to God. His eyes were sensitive from his illness and medication, and the white stone reflection hurt them.

"God, if I may address you like that here, I imagine lives don't matter to you, as we all die. I beg you for a delay of ten years, only ten more years, please, and I will study your scriptures every day that I continue to live."

He kissed the sun-warmed rocks. He saw notes written on paper in the cracks. Should I write one? he thought. And in what language? My English is not that good. Should I write in Croatian? Of course, God knows all the languages, but maybe German would be more convincing, being so close to Yiddish. *Gott sei Dank fuer meinen Leben.*

On the way back, they walked around the walls to Herod's gate and, not far from it, Davor saw a sign: the Garden of the Tomb. "What tomb?" he asked when they got close to it.

"The tomb of Jesus," the person at the door said. "Would you like the map? In what language?"

"Croatian."

"Yes, we have it. Here you go, God bless you."

Inside, he asked a preacher, "How is this possible? We just spent a whole day at the tomb of Jesus, and you say this is it? I don't remember him being in two tombs."

"We believe this is the real one," the tall Englishman with yellow teeth said. "You know the city was destroyed, so nobody really knows where the original walls were; the Ottomans outlined the city differently when they built the current walls. In the nineteenth century, several British archaeologists figured out that the real tomb was here."

Alana and Davor walked around the grounds, admiring their simplicity without massive gold and silver and rubies. The tomb of Jesus had an antechamber and two parallel graves, which were at most five feet long. "Was Jesus five feet tall?" asked Davor. "Otherwise, he would have had to crouch in the grave. That would be something, a five-foot-long God. Well, Beethoven was less than five feet tall."

"Look," Alana said, "the stones here contain streaks of red."

"Oh, that's just iron, don't worry about it," said an English preacher. "You don't need miracles to believe if you are inclined to believe."

"How can there be two tombs?" Davor said. "Maybe there's a third one, like a real biblical number. And what difference does it make when he was in one of them for only three days. It's like a hotel. It's like houses in Russia. Here stayed Lenin for three days."

Alana wept. "This is it, it looks so real. This is where he was dead and where he rose from the dead. It's obvious."

"What's suddenly come over you?" Davor asked.

A couple of big blind men held hands and prayed in tongues under a canopy, and on the side a Russian group sang gospel in squeaky voices, many out of tune, adding a note of despair. The Golgotha here indeed looked like a skull (overlooking a gas station and an Arab bus terminal with green and white buses), and that was the original meaning of the Golgotha, the Skull, and it was higher than the Golgotha in the church of the Holy Sepulcher. This one appealed to the minimalist and purist protestant aesthetics, and the older Holy Sepulcher appealed to Orthodox and Catholic Baroque tastes.

"These are just the visual aids for your faith," the English preacher who kept shadowing them said. "You can choose which one works better for you. For me, this is better. I don't have to dig through all the gold and the tourist fanfare to get to the image of the tombstone and the stone covering the tomb."

"Oh, really?" Davor asked. "So this is like a theater of faith?"

"If you want to put it that way, yes."

Now all that was left was the Dome on the Rock, or the Holy of Holies. Orthodox Jews weren't allowed to go there, by their own religion. You should not walk into the Holy of Holies.

At the gate, a guard with a machine gun said to Alana, "You aren't allowed to go in with your ankles bare. We could get you decent shoes and socks."

"You go ahead," she told Davor. "I'll wait for you right here."

Davor loved the sight of Mt. Moriah and marveled at the sensation of the forbidden and inaccessible. Only between 2:30 and 3:30 in the afternoon were non-Muslims allowed to come in past the Arab-Israeli guards.

Nobody knew exactly where the Holy of Holies was, but it was somewhere near the Dome on the Rock. Davor read in the tourist guide that the King of Jordan put eighty-five million dollars of gold into the dome and that was when gold was twelve times less expensive than now. In other words, the dome contained one billion dollars worth of gold. But never mind that. The soil contained the blood of more than a million pilgrims, Muslims, and Jews fighting for that square kilometer of arid land. He shivered at the thought, and then imagined what would happen if he stepped right into the Holy of Holies somewhere near the blue-tiled golden mosque. Would he puff into nothing? Many Orthodox Jews feared that, but how many of them could actually believe that? I mean, really, who could?

"Sir, are you Muslim?" asked a young man at the entrance to the Dome.

"Yes," Davor said. He was surprised he so readily lied, but why would he deny himself the foundation rock, the oldest rock on earth, from which the rest of the earth was created? "From Bosnia."

"Welcome, brother," said the man, and Davor took off his shoes and slowly walked in. While his eyes were adjusting in the dark, he smelled lots of socks, socks that had been in shoes in the hot weather for a long time, socks of pilgrims afflicted with athlete's foot, who had spent days getting here like himself, and he nearly fainted. He turned around, put on his shoes, and walked out.

How could Holy of Holies be in the fumes of overheated feet? Davor wondered. Now it made sense that Jesus would want his feet washed and oiled, though of course he didn't walk around in Adidas sneakers.

At the end of the day, he and Alana were having dinner, Dennis fish, in the garden near the hotel, and he kept looking at the limestone wall. It had the same red streaks as the stone beneath the Golgotha in the Holy Sepulcher. The streaks were common.

"Look, this is all a bunch of bullshit," he said. "There are red stains in the rocks here all over the place. It's not the blood of Jesus, and there's no foundation rock of the earth here, and it's all just a bunch of bull."

"What's come over you, why are you angry?" Alana asked.

"Why wouldn't I be angry?"

"You should be happy, we are in the Holy Land. I find it wonderful. I believe in God now."

"Guess what? I no longer do."

"What?"

"My faith just evaporated here. It's a bunch of steam that vanished in the dry air. Nothing's left in my head but death. Maybe I've stepped into the Holy of Holies and this is part of my death, puffing into nothing like cigarette smoke."

"If we hadn't come here, you'd still believe?"

"Certainly."

"But you can't give up on faith now, now that you really need it."

"And that's another reason why I give up on it. I don't want to believe out of despair."

"Out of hope."

"It's the same thing. If you hope, you also despair. If you despair, you also hope. I feel nothing about the beyond. I don't fucking care."

"Watch your language, you are in the Holy Land."

"Oh yeah? How holy is it to herd people behind one tall wall? It's twice as tall as the wall in Berlin, you've seen it below Mt. Olive. And you saw that sign, *Ich bin Ein Berliner*. What's holy in ghettoizing poor people? What's holy in repeating the historical mistakes? Don't do unto others as...well, as was done unto them? This place is full of lies. Even the stones lie. All three religions lie."

"Hey, quiet, calm down."

"I have no reason to be quiet. I still have some breath left and some brain, not much, so let me at least vent my belief, my lack of belief. And if I commit sacrilege, what will happen? I will die like a dog. You know what, I'm already dying like a dog. And I don't want to live in a world where a bloody city like this counts as Holy of Holies. This is the best we can come up with, all this blood?"

"Oh my God, how can you talk like that? You're frightening me."

"Sorry, I know, it's not fair. You've been so patient with me. Forgive me. But now that you have a friend in Jesus, you're all set. You'll never be lonely."

"You're right. I am so happy, and I'll pray for you."

When they returned from Israel to Zagreb, they encountered a cold wave of weather, a slanted rain with a bit of sleet in it. Davor caught a chill and fever just from being out in the rain for a few minutes as they walked to the airport parking lot.

His condition worsened quickly. He no longer read the Bible or anything, as the letters shifted and swirled in his vision. He only watched soccer, although he repeatedly muttered to himself, "I don't care who wins, I don't know these people, they are too rich anyway, how can I want any good to happen to a rich person." And then he'd fall asleep. Strangely enough, he woke up and couldn't get out of bed. He could barely lift his head, but not much.

He moaned in pain. His head hurt, his bones hurt, his chest hurt.

He was taken to the hospital for an exam, and the findings were that his cancer had progressed, that it was metastasis, and now it affected his bones and his brain. He had a series of small strokes. It was hard to explain, the doctors said. His moaning became louder, and doctors administered high doses of morphine. And he didn't pray, didn't even say "Oh God." He swore like a Turk, like a Croat. And then the ambulance returned him home.

Upon seeing the red bricks of his home, he laughed. "And whose blood is this in the bricks? Is it mine? Is it the blood of the Serbs killed in the Second World War here?" His dog sniffed him and barked as though he'd become someone else in the meantime.

Now that he was bedridden, and the doctors determined that another wave of chemo would only be detrimental at this point, the only thing that could help would be hemp oil and morphine. His old friends and relatives began to visit. They all quieted down, unsure of whether he was still conscious, whether he was asleep or awake, and he wasn't sure whether he was asleep or awake, whether this was part of some methodical nightmare that, although boring, grew more and more dreadful by the hour. Nights were especially harrowing, with hallucinations and wheezing.

As morning doves began to coo on his roof, announcing the thinning of the night, dispersing the darkness (where did it all go, where could it hide in this universe that is mostly darkness?), he felt relief and wondered whether his nicotine-stained teeth hurt, and if they did, whether he would notice toothache among the many other shades of ache he suffered. He could not get out of bed, could not lift his head, and Alana tilted him to one side and the other to wipe and wash him as though he were already a corpse, or Jesus taken off the cross. But no, he didn't want to think of the religious metaphor because he didn't believe, but the fact that his cessation of belief had precipitated such a swift decline tempted him to believe again. Maybe it was divine retribution, and that it was so effective suggested God's power at work.

His cousins came. A doctor who worked as a cardiologist in Zagreb and his younger brother Mirko, a journalist for the Croatian daily, *Vecernji list, Abendblatt.* Davor suddenly remembered how he'd taught Mirko, who was four years younger, to masturbate in order to make his penis grow when the boy was eleven years old. "Do it every day. If you don't do it every day, it won't grow, and trust me, you want to have an above-average penis if you want to be loved by a beautiful woman."

Poor shmuck, he thought and smiled, and neither of them have any idea what I am thinking now. He opened one eye and peered at Mirko, who had grown a big beard since he'd last visited a year before, looking like Moses or Karl Marx. Or God. Not Jesus, Jesus didn't have an impressive beard.

His wife said, "His mind is going. He called from the hospital and said, 'I don't see anything.' I was scared that he'd lost his sight, but he meant to say, 'I don't hear anything.' The words mix up. Lucky thing he can see."

"But he can't hear?"

"Usually he can't. Sometimes he has a phase when he can hear a little."

"The brain is a miraculous thing," said the doctor.

"How long do you think he has to live?" asked Mirko. "Seven days? Nine?"

"I don't know. It's not easy to predict such things," the doctor replied.

"He looks weak, but somehow happy and clever."

The doctor bared Davor's shins and pressed them with his thumb, and said, "The legs are a normal temperature and there's no swelling whatsoever, so it means the heart and the kidneys are doing their job despite his not moving at all. With a good heart, there's no telling how long he could last. It could be months, unless, of course, his brain suddenly shuts down the impulses through the life center."

Davor heard and understood all of this but, with the excess of morphine in his body, all he could do was grimace vaguely and good-naturedly. His wife commented, "Oh, he's so sweet sometimes, like a baby. You can see it, there's bliss in his face."

Both visitors shook his right hand and kissed him on the cheeks and on the forehead, then left. Oh yes, shake my masturbating hand, he thought. I will probably never do it again, and I'll never have sex again. He suddenly felt abandoned; he knew that these were Judas's kisses, absolving them of further duty to visit him ever again. This was the last time. Fuckers.

Then came a parade of his former alcoholic friends, some with beards, others bald, some fat, some thin, some smelling of tobacco, some of hay and shit and urine and sperm. His sense of smell increased as his sight decreased. And they all felt sorry for him, some even seemed to weep, but he got a sense that all of them also looked at his wife hungrily. She was sexy, fifteen years younger than him, and most of them were such lousy friends that they would probably paw and fuck her on his deathbed. In the tone of her voice, he sometimes thought he noticed some flirtation. And anyhow, they hadn't had sex in months, ever since Purim in Tel Aviv. In Jerusalem, they had forgotten about sex, so knocked out by heat and pilgrimage. Oh, he hadn't even known it was the last time and, then, even as he was making love to her, he wasn't quite there, but imagining some nearly naked girl with torn stockings and thick red lips he'd seen in the streets of Tel Aviv.

His Czech cousins, ten years older than him, also came. One of them was a mechanical engineer who'd spent ten years in Cuba and who could never make it through a conversation without mentioning the wonders of Cuba. And sure enough, after going through the usual *It's so sad* spiel, he began saying, "When we landed in Havana…" Davor didn't want to hear the rest. He wanted to be asleep, wanted this man to be out of his life, and for himself to be gone out of his life.

And then his sister visited from Sweden. She'd worked as a nurse there. But now because of back pains, she was semi-retired. She loved to talk about death and tragedy, and he had a sense that she kind of enjoyed it, as long as it was others and not she who was dying.

His sister and his wife talked for a long time while he writhed in pain. He asked for morphine, but who knows what came out of his mouth. He could not count on words coming out in the right order, and he couldn't count on his thoughts making sense. There was silence. He couldn't hear them. Maybe he shrieked, he didn't know. He felt chilly, and the pain that amassed in his head and bones and abdomen was sharp and fiery; he'd eaten flames that couldn't be put out. His head hurt as though a primitive dentist was cutting off his frontal lobe and, for all he knew, maybe that was happening, maybe someone was performing surgery to remove part of his brain, the amygdala perhaps. And maybe his cancer had already eaten the amygdala, or had instead made it grow like a pear. The pain and the pressure in his brain were such that he grabbed his head with his hands and sat up.

"Oh, he's better," said his sister. "Look, he has some strength. He's risen."

"Praise the Lord," said his wife. "He has risen!"

He saw the women clearly and felt lucid, and could hear and smell everything again, but he could not get rid of or reach the pain. His half-blond, half-gray sister with thick-framed glasses, which magnified her eyes, stared at him like a horned owl he remembered from his childhood.

"Is there any more morphine?" Davor asked with startling clarity.

"You've had your dose for the evening," said Alana.

"Oh really? Give me more. I am in pain."

"We'll have to get some more in the morning. You're out."

"Out?"

"Yeah, just sleep till the morning. We'll get you plenty."

"That's easy for you to say," he said.

"Look how clearly he speaks. He's better," said his sister.

"You shut up, you old owl!"

"Maybe he's not better," Alana said.

"Will you stop this bullshit," he said. "All this pity, and I don't even have a decent painkiller. I'll show you what pain is, you sorry assholes."

Davor jumped out of bed, grabbed a chair, and smashed it on the floor. It was an old chair, left over from his grandfather's business. His grandfather had been a chairmaker in Pecs, Hungary. "Sorry, Grandpa," he said, and smashed the leg stick still left in his hand over an earthenware flowerpot, which cracked.

His sister shrieked.

"Just you shriek," he said, and punched her in the face so hard that she flew to the wall, hitting it with the back of her head. "That will teach you to feel sorry for me. What gives you the right, you smug owl?"

"Don't be like that. What did she do to you? She loves you," said Alana.

"Fuck love like this. I'm tired of all the sympathy, you hypocrites. I'm tired of all your Schadenfreude. You love it that I'm dying. You'll inherit this whole bloody house, and it's soulful and ennobling to watch someone die, isn't it? Now you're even close to Jesus, your best pal. Which one? The one from the golden pink-marble tomb or the one from the plain limestone tomb?"

He kicked Alana and then hit her, tearing the skin on her left cheekbone.

He chased the two women around the house and, in the middle of the chase, he attained a sense of wellbeing and near ecstasy. His pain was gone, and all his senses were as sharp as ever, he was young and strong, and he loved listening to them scream. Their screams matched the best orgasms he'd heard in the best of his lovemaking. Their screams proved that he was young and strong and in control. He wouldn't chase them for long—just a few more minutes. It was better than lying around and dying. This was life.

They locked themselves in the closet and called an ambulance. Two male nurses arrived and Davor shouted at them. "I know what brings you here. You want to whore around with these two sluts."

The nurses tried to subdued him, but he punched one of them in the face. While Davor flipped tables and kicked in the TV screen, they called the cops. He picked up the TV and tossed it through the glass window, into the street.

The police hit him over the head with a billy club.

"Wait a minute, that's not cool," Alana said. "He has brain cancer, and he's had strokes."

"Sorry, how else can we calm him down? Shoot him? Or you want us to leave him alone till he kills you?"

The cops handcuffed Davor and placed him in the ambulance, then drove him to the hospital in Slavonski Brod. There, he was heavily medicated and he passed out into fluffy dreams.

Alana and his sister visited, and played old Gospel music for him. The two of them sang:

Amazing Grace, how sweet the sound,
That saved a wretch like me...
I once was lost but now am found,
Was blind, but now I see.

They all had tears in their eyes, and he smiled blissfully, or so he thought. He knew he was losing his brain, and the vague sounds from his past still didn't resurrect Christ for him. Christ had many graves, two in Israel and thousands everywhere, and he would stay in the ground for more than three days—maybe three thousand years. Davor thought about Christ the man; he still didn't believe in the God. But then he thought, what do I know? And what difference does it make whether I know something or don't, whether I believe or not? Should I be saved based on my opinions, and if my opinion is that there's no God and no salvation, and then there is a God, should he care about my opinion one way or another? Should the opinion of a damaged brain matter? If this is all his doing, even not believing in him is a form of celebrating him. And then, who needs celebrations? I've kind of celebrated, and it's embarrassing; I'm sorry I inflicted pain on the ones who love me. I didn't think they loved me, but look, they've forgiven me everything, and they're playing this lame music from my childhood, ditties about love and God. It is touching, and I wish I could talk, but I can't open my mouth, can't lift my hand, I am done for, I'm surprised I can think, if this is thinking. And look, their tears are falling onto me. Well, I can't cry and weep, what would be the point, and what's the point of asking for points. It's all over.

He thought he heard a doctor say, "We can't do anything for him anymore. We have plenty of morphine for him, and you can take him home. He's all yours. There's nothing more we can do."

The two male nurses and two women in his life, his wife and his sister, took him home, where he lay for three days and three nights and then died with a mysterious half-smile on his thin blue lips, his blue eyes pale like the spring sky, irises only, with tiny and hazed-over pupils, reduced to milky black dots bleeding into the blue.

HERITAGE OF SMOKE

Jovan brushed his teeth, had a glass of cold water, and inhaled deeply. The water tasted a bit metallic, as though it had come through rusty pipes, but maybe it was his bleeding gums. He spat out white spittle, so it wasn't his gums. He shaved the top half of his moustache, turning what remained into a Spanish-style pencil.

It was wonderful to not smoke. After three years of freedom, he smelled the pine needles outside his window. He smelled all sorts of flowers—he closed his eyes and tried to sort them out. Even in Batajnica, the woeful suburbs of Belgrade, it was possible to enjoy the spring. God may have forsaken the Balkan people, but not its nature, which seemed to bloom all the more vigorously after the recent evils.

The phone rang. He picked up the receiver and immediately recognized the voice of his second cousin, Danko. "Amazing to hear from you. It's been, what, five years since I saw you last," he said.

"More. I'd say eight, since 1991."

"How come you remembered me just now?"

"Well, it's a bad news, good news kind of thing. Which do you want first?

"I haven't had any good news in ages. I wouldn't understand. So, give me the bad news."

"Your uncle Dusan killed himself."

"Mother. Really? How?"

"Hanged himself with a rope at the farmer's market. I guess he liked the metal beams there. He'd tried once before from a crossbeam in the vineyards, but the rotten beam cracked and knocked him on the head, giving him a concussion."

"Do you know why he did it? Did he leave a note?"

"No idea why. Maybe no external reason. This suicide bug runs in our families, doesn't it? Like your brother killing himself four years ago. You must still be in pain over that memory."

"He drank a bottle of brandy a day, he felt nothing and could think nothing. Who could, after so much alcohol? So if he felt nothing and thought nothing, why should I feel anything for him?"

"That's a strange thing to say."

"Only strange things are worth saying. What do you want me to do, follow a script and weep? I went through that too, years ago, but this being in exile, cut off from home, you know, this has taught me some stoicism. But let's not psychoanalyze now. Tell me more about Dusan."

"It's probably a genetic destiny in our family, so I don't really know much except that, lately, he lived with all sorts of doves and pigeons, you know, like you used to."

"So who's taking care of the doves now?"

"There's a friend of his, Milan, who'll take care of them. He inherited them. Dusan wrote a note, donating his doves to Milan, and here comes the good news. He listed you and me as inheritors of the house in Vinogradi. What do you suggest we do?"

"Really, the house still exists? I thought the local Ustashas would have blown it up."

"You don't have to believe your local propaganda."

"Well, I can't use the house. I'm never coming back."

"Anyway, I already found a buyer, some Italian who came over to hunt boars. You know that's the new tourism in Papuk and Psunj, boar hunting. He'll give us 22,000 euros. So let's split it, like brothers."

"Sounds good, if the house is not firm enough to hang yourself from its beams. Yes, sounds good, splitting, except for the brothers part. So half and half? Eleven grand for me."

"The house has good beams. It's the vineyard beams that are rotten. No, ten for you, and twelve for me. A bit of commission, as I have to sell and deal with all sorts of legality. And I'll bring you the money, in cash, next week, if that's all right with you. So I do all this work, bring it to you, and you just get it in your hands, no tax, nothing."

"Yes, of course it's all right. Here I am practically starving with my family, house needs finishing, ten grand, yes."

"Are you coming to the funeral? It's going to be a cremation next Wednesday."

"No, I haven't been to Croatia in all these years. And what good would it do Dusan? He won't know who shows up."

"All the more reason to visit—you must be nostalgic. War shit is one thing, but your native landscape is another."

"I'll come after all the wars are over."

"You might wait for a while, then."

"Or at least until after NATO bombs us again."

"You're sure they will?"

"I listen to the BBC. Maybe ten days at the most."

"Can you talk like that on the phone? Are you sure it's not bugged?"

"I don't give a shit if it is. What can they do to me? Throw me out of Serbia? I wouldn't mind—they can send me to Sweden.

But if you're coming here, do it as soon as you can. It might be hard once the bombing begins."

"You really believe it will happen?"

"Come here and we'll talk. And bring some Slavonian sljiva."

"Sure, if you bring some Sumadijska loza."

Two days after this conversation, Jovan walked out of his house down a narrow street in a light rain. At least it had been asphalted the year before. These used to be sunflower fields there, but Milosevic had allowed peasants to sell their fields for real estate developments, and it had been pretty cheap, so Jovan had bought a plot alongside many other refugees from Croatia and Bosnia and slowly brick-laid his house with his wife's help. Bricks were cheap, as there was plenty of clay under the green earth, and it just had to be baked right in the kilns. He was tempted to do it alone, dig up the earth and bake it, but then he'd have to fill in the holes (or leave them for a fish pond) and it would have all taken too long, so he bought these hollowed-out bricks, the new fashion. As a child, he'd helped his father brick-lay their house, and the bricks then used to be solid, like a brick so to speak, but now air insulation in the bricks would accomplish more to keep them all warm than a solid brick would. Who knew air was that good? On the other hand, the old brick walls could take grenade hits better, and in the Balkans that mattered. Still, you could hardly find the old-style solid bricks anymore.

As the town had expanded without a plan, and many of the exiled peasants wanted as much yard as possible to maximize their plot (they gardened and kept chickens and goats), little land remained for the streets, which were basically paths that were too narrow to bring in city buses, and so it took fifteen minutes of brisk walking to get to the first bus stop or the train station. Before being asphalted, the paths used to melt into mud during the rainy seasons, and Jovan and his children would trudge through the mud with plastic bags around their shoes. Before they started using bags, his children kept losing shoes; the mud sucked them in, and sometimes it seemed the mud would even suck his children into the earth, drown and bury them. Walking through it was quite a struggle, worse than walking through deep snow, but that too could be challenging in the winter, with snowdrifts blown across from the flat fields of Vojvodina, maybe even Hungary, so that one winter their house, one of the first wind-breaks north of Belgrade, got completely buried in snow, and he'd had to shovel a tunnel out of the house to get his children to school. As he believed in education, he did this even on the worst days, having come from three generations of schoolteachers. He used to be a history teacher too, in Croatia, but in Serbia nobody needed histories anymore. If you need history, hell, we'll make history, right here in Serbia, seemed to be the attitude. And we Serbs are so misunderstood, there's no hope of anyone understanding us right, so why read anyone and their hateful venom? This kind of Serbian imperviousness to analyzing history annoyed Jovan so much that he concluded he wasn't a patriot.

Anyway, he didn't mind walking down these paths; he could think here more than anywhere else, and it always refreshed him to see that there wasn't a single bar in the entire town settlement. People drank at home to save money, and exiles mistrusted strangers and preferred to be home, behind double-locked doors, with a growling German Shepherd on the porch. Jovan despised alcoholism in general and Balkan soddenness especially, and seeing no group drunkenness in the neighborhood, no matter what the miserable causes of that were, comforted him.

Occasionally thin, lonely men, whose wives beat them if they drank too much, stood outside the few corner stores and drank their half-liter Jelen beers. It was all so wet that smoking cigarettes used to give him an illusion of being warm and dry. Today the drizzle chilled him and made him nostalgic for smoke. He looked around and sighed with satisfaction: no Serbian flags anywhere. Who says Serbs are nationalists? The fact that they did not appear to be nationalistic gave him a surge of national pride. No Cyrillic lettering in sight. These were supposed to be patriotic Serbs here, but most of them got disillusioned fast with the way the government ghettoized them, gave them the worst jobs, recruited their sons for the army, and so out of quiet protest there were no flags out here and most people kept their old customs and ways of talking instead of adapting Serbian ways.

On the bus, he didn't validate his ticket out of habit, as ninety dinars would suffice for a burek, good enough for lunch. Of course, if he got 10,000 euros—he still didn't believe he would, it was preposterous!—he could afford to pay the fare. Hardly anybody paid it, and people looked more alert than they normally would be—they all needed more sleep—because they were on the lookout for the controller. Once the controller came on at the next stop, half the bus would jump out, and the other half would quickly validate their tickets, and one sucker would get stuck with the fine.

In downtown Belgrade, Jovan leaned against the pink marble of the Hotel Moskva, next to the Fountain Square, and looked out past the red potted flowers. He wasn't sure what the name of the flower was, but the sunshine made it as beautiful as new blood. There had been a protest here against Milosevic a few weeks before, but it hadn't done any good.

He looked down at his soiled boots. He had bought them for one euro at the flea market, as he had his purple turtleneck, black leather jacket, and blue jeans. He joked that he was a one-euro man, as each item on him cost one euro. It was quarter to two. Danko had promised he would come at two. He had no cellphone that worked abroad, Danko had said, and for that matter Jovan didn't have a cellphone either. He'd never yet had a phone call that bore good news. The less news, the better. And why would anybody call him?

But in this case, he thought, it would be useful. Jovan sat down at a café and ordered. "A coffee!" He didn't say please. What would be the point? If the waiter didn't bring him anything, it would be just as fine. In fact, Jovan hated spending money.

"What kind of coffee?" asked the waiter.

"What do you mean, what kind? Coffee is coffee."

"Well, there's macchiato, cappuccino, espresso…"

"Just coffee. Call it Turkish if you like."

"There's Turkish coffee, but there's also Americano, which…"

"Give me Turkish coffee, then." And he thought, what's the world come to that you need to call the same thing by different names? Bosnian, Serbian, Montenegrin, Croatian…despite different names and accents and folklore, aren't we all the same? How can coffee have so many nationalities? It's still the same damned bitter mud.

The brown coffee smudge came in a small long-handled copper vessel, which shone like gold, accompanied by a tiny cup of Lomonosov blue porcelain with golden trim. Jovan put a cube of sugar into the coffee, waited for the floating layer of coffee grains to sink, and sipped reluctantly, wondering what to think about. Pigeons jerkily drank water at the fountain, and the sun gave them a blue and purple sheen, so that you could mistake them for doves.

2:15. Danko is not here yet, Jovan realized and looked around, without taking off his leather jacket. Oh well, with how the trains work, it's no surprise. Who knows when the train from Budapest arrives. In Tito's time, the *Poslovni vlak* only took four hours between Zagreb and Belgrade, and the engineers planned to cut it to two with the first TGV train in the world. The project never materialized, and now it takes at least fourteen hours, as one has to change trains and go to a different train station, in a Nordic loop.

2:30. The pigeons are gone for some reason, but where is Danko? And my coffee is cold, and those two buskers I remember from last year are back, singing their Vojvodina depression. *Kada padne prvi sneg. When the first snow falls...*

2:50. Now that's a little excessive—fifty minutes late. He said his train would arrive at 2:05, which means even if he were in the last coach, he should make it up to the Fountain Square twenty minutes later. And Hungarians are not all that relaxed, they wouldn't let their trains be late for hours like the gelatinous Slovenes and Croats do. I don't know why "gelatinous" popped up in my mind. Maybe I hate the southwest Slavs. Anyway, do I really hate anyone? Is that a character flaw that I don't nourish my hatreds?

3:00. That's an entire hour of tardiness. Is he coming? Maybe he doesn't know Belgrade? Maybe Danko asked for directions and some ill-intentioned bum sent him the wrong way on account of his accent?

3:01. What if I'm completely wrong and nothing good is going to happen? What if no uncle died? Why do I believe everything I hear? What if it's a practical joke? Some bozo called to tease me? Do I have any enemies left in Daruvar? Who would hate me? Is that bad that I believe that nobody really hates me? Was I so inconsequential that nobody bothered to love or hate me—other than my wife whom I imported here, and my children who are doomed by biology to love me through a kind of desperate bribe for protection?

3:13. This crazy wind is blowing dust, I'm sneezing, and no first, second, or third cousins in sight. Well, third cousins probably. That would be five degrees of separation, and isn't the entire continent separated by a maximum of six degrees? But whoever came up with that formula meant people knowing each other, not necessarily sharing the same fucking genes. In any case, where the hell is this second cousin? With the mixed marriages, he's actually Croatian. I can't even be sure of his name. Danko may be short for Danimir, basically a bad translation of Theodore.

3:45. This is horrifying. I could handle things like these when I smoked. But I never had things like these, I was never in a position to wait for a relative stranger, or stranger relative, who would just hand over 10,000 euro. Why would he do it? *a)* He's executor of the will, *b)* he's a good man, *c)* he's a retard. Now what if there's a *d)* none of the above? Well then, he'll look at the red and pink money and say, "Fuck this Jovan. He can't even bother to visit Croatia to claim an inheritance. I'll buy a cottage on the Drava River just south of Hungary and fish for trout and catfish and carp, and make fantastic fish paprikash. So yes, fuck him."

3:46. For heaven's sake! That woman near the piano crosses her legs better than Brigitte Bardot. Is she Serbian? Croatian? Russian? The lines of her legs are fabulous in their clarity and simplicity. I bet that's how Picasso founded triangulism. Sure, they called it cubism, but there's not a single fucking cube in his work. Not even a proper square. It's all triangles. He was a dirty old man, but why was he so dirty? He was a man looking for life, the first guiding light for the armies of spermatozoa that propagate life. So how dirty is it to obey life? Not obeying life and death and rotting is even dirtier. Oh, I'm just distracting myself. Danko is still not here. Danke Deutschland. Where does the name Danko come from? Now, how much would I give to make love to this triangulating beauty? But why should it cost me anything? The entire inheritance. Now that would be the height of stupidity. But then, why not? At this point, I would like to kill myself. Why wouldn't I? Half of my family has ended their lives in suicide. That means they were all philosophical like the Wittgensteins. They loved suicide. Why not blow 10,000 euros for one moment of fulfillment? I'm surprised I haven't jumped off a cliff or a twentieth floor balcony yet. I lean over, and I just think how wonderful it would be to smash on the pavement below. The second before hitting the ground would be ecstatic terror. Now really...this is all nonsense. I won't look at her.

He looked at the black piano next to her across the room of marble floors. Is it a Steinway? He couldn't see the lettering from the glare of the sun, which bounced off a window across the street, hit the varnish, and ricocheted to the woman's underwear, yes, definitely blue, Lomonosov blue.

3:67. I don't want to think it's already past four. Of course, that's all I am thinking, other than that sensational thigh, which she still hasn't budged. How can she sit in the same pose for so long? What if she gets a vein clot, thrombosis? I would. It's like flying trans-Atlantic. You've got to move as much as you can or you'll end up crippled. No circulation, the foot swells, bacteria has enough time to multiply in one location, and voila, chop the foot off, that's the only way out. Now how come medicine has not advanced? They still amputate.

3:68. You'd imagine, nowadays, we'd be in better shape, and not need amputations. But that's peripheral. Where is Danko?

4:15. How she smokes! Small mouth, nearly a circle, with her swell lips. How come nobody has formed an Oism movement? Circulism? It would be so much more life-promoting than cubism. Sharp angles, sharp lines…but a curve forever, isn't that what it's all about? About, around, round? Yes, I'm founding the movement of circulism. Now, why don't I talk to her? What could I say? May I light your cigarette? It's much worse than that. May I suck on your cigarette, just once, before I die? Is that true, I will never taste or inhale nicotine? That sounds way too final. Yes, why don't I go to her and ask, "Madame, may I bum a cigarette from you?" It's actually not about sex, but smoking.

4:21. This Slobodan Milosevic, plum brandy banker, why the hell did he happen? Now we have borders, and maybe Danko is in jail because it's illegal to carry so much cash. Nearly all Milosevic's ancestors committed suicide. Why hasn't he? There were at least ten attempts on his life, fifty on Tito's, a hundred on Hitler's. Now, what bad luck, to try so many times and not succeed. This guy Kavaja, an Albanian Serb—now that's a breed—tried to kill Tito four times and failed. And boasted of failure. And became an international celebrity for failing. What a jerk. Fake, no doubt. Just a talker. I wonder how much history we read from fake boasters.

4:22. Man, the smoke coming out of her lips! No, not out of the lips, that would be sick, but out of her oral cavity. Now that sounds too medical, and there's nothing good about the medical issues when the oral cavity is in question. It's a disaster zone, and this beautiful disaster zone, Masha's mouth—yes, she must be Russian, just look at her lips, and this is after all Hotel Moskva—what glistening heaven it is.

4:25. I kind of spaced out on my last question. Danko is not here. I think I'm a fool. Or idiot. What is better? Choose the worse form. Idiot is blessed by definition. I'm cursed. Hence, I'm a fool.

4:26. I pretend to be a thinker, but the fact is I'm a sore non-smoker.

4:27. Alcoholics have it better. They may abstain from booze for thirty years, yet they are still alcoholics. I haven't smoked for three years, and I'm already a non-smoker. Fuck it. It's not fair. I should smoke.

4:28:37. Why am I here? What can I think about it? A lot. But why? Why is always in front of every thought. It's Spanish grammar. The thought is always preceded by a question mark. Why figure out only in the end that you are asking? If you are asking, don't you know you are shitting asking? Why isn't "shitting" a preferred adverb to fucking? Nobody understands "shitting asking," but "fucking asking" sounds natural.

??? I don't know what shitty time this is.

4:something. Where the shit is this imaginary Second Cousin?

4:30. Well, properly speaking, it's only been two and a half hours since the date with the deliverer of the proceeds of death, my second cousin. We are shameless vultures, devouring our own bloody relatives.

4:31. I don't know. I don't know. Why don't I at least think?

4:32. Her thighs are glistening and tanned. From the Adriatic coast? Maybe she's Croatian or Russian vacationing in Croatia. Holy smoke. I will ask her. I will. In French, German, Russian, Serbian. What else do I speak. Croatian. What a joke. Is that a dialect, language? I affirm, it's not even a dialect. It's some kind of artificial merging of Serbian and dialects, a fraud.

4:32. Why is so much packed in this moment? Yes, lots is lost in this minute. I will kill this Danko. Do I have a gun? I am a night watchman for a Swedish security firm and I don't even have a fucking gun. What kind of Serb am I?

4:33. I admit it. Time is passing. It's all about passing and none about retention. Where is time now? Is the present moment a miniscule, 0 seconds? We don't exist in time but between time, a nothing sandwiched in dual infinities.

4:38. I don't know why it took me so long to think of this: I am getting nothing. Some guy got hold of my number and teased me, playing my greed note. Greed is a note on the scale of emotions that can be played. Maybe all emotions can be used, but greed foremost.

5:05. It's a pretty number, 505.

5:06. Holy smoke. How can I just wait? What a fool I am. At least if I had something to do, but how could I concentrate on anything now? I could always think of the money. The only way to be distracted is to smoke. I haven't smoked in ages, maybe just this one time. It will be functional. It will kill time. So what if it kills me slowly. But I can't take this time. Thinking about time is already killing me, and it's not killing time. But if I run across the street to the kiosk, I might miss Danko, and he might think that I have already given up. If if.

5:07. Maybe I should ask that tall waiter to bring me a pack? But he would charge ten times more. Oh, I'll ask this man to sell me one for ten dinars. For ten dinars you could get three, I think.

"Izvinite, can I please buy a cigarette off of you?"

"Why would you buy it? You can have one."

"God bless you!"

I don't believe in God, but then I should thank him somehow, and just the basic thank you didn't seem to be emphatic enough. "But, you know, one may not be enough, I'm waiting and waiting for..."

"Here, have two of them, then."

The young man struck a match and lit Jovan's cigarette. Jovan inhaled deep. Heaven. How could I live without it?

"What kind of cigarette is it?" Jovan asked.

"Ronhill."

"But that's from Rovinj, in Croatia. How did it get here? Can't we roll our own tobacco?"

"Some things don't change."

The young man walked away, and Jovan inhaled again. The warm smoke spread, filled his lungs, and suddenly he felt clear-headed. The cloud of months of rainy weather and wars and rumors of wars and death camps lifted, and now he could think. Danko was bringing the money and was delayed at the border near Subotica, Jovan surmised. Maybe the cops discovered Danko had that much cash and stole it from him. Maybe he passed through and will tell me that the border police confiscated the money but let him go generously as he didn't know that it was a crime to carry more than what the fuck is the sum, 3,000 euros, in cash? God, what chance do I have of getting this money? Either the cops will steal the money, or Danko will lie that the money was stolen, or he simply won't show up, or maybe he was turned away at the border and he will have enough time to think of it, and will conclude that he likes himself better than me, that he could buy a vineyard of Riesling in the hills outside of Daruvar with 10,000 euros.

Put yourself in his shoes, Jovan thought, maybe shoes worn on the outer edges, with swollen ankles from spraining in various potholes. Why would he bring me the money?

And so Jovan smoked and then bought a pack of cigarettes from the Hotel Balkan across the street. At the Balkan, cigarettes weren't all that overpriced, and Jovan smoked Drina, named after his favorite river, favorite because he loved Ivo Andric. At 5:30 he thought, why am I here, still waiting? He has my address, and if he comes ten hours later, he can find me at home. He can afford to pay for a cab ride. I am done. Okay, just one more minute. Oh wait, is that him?

Jovan saw a man about his age with a French beret, a leather jacket, a yellow moustache and yellow fingers, and a briefcase. Danko? Yes, Danko!

The two men hugged briefly and vigorously.

Danko said, "You haven't changed much, other than that you don't have that much hair on top."

"Oh, hair loss is nothing new," Jovan replied. "All I was going to lose, I already did in Daruvar."

"Well, now you'll have enough money to buy Rogaine if you want to regrow your hair."

"I don't believe in that crap, plus I am fine like this. I don't have to worry about combing, and if I'm cold, I wear a hat."

"And you still smoke the same way!"

"To tell you the truth, I just started smoking again while waiting for you. I don't actually smoke. This is just an exception. After a while I wasn't sure you were coming. And you are smoking too."

"The trains were so late, and the borders make me nervous, so I started again. This is my first smoke in six months."

"Holy smoke! Maybe our inheritance is not so much money as it is smoke. Our suicidal relative left us a smoking habit. But I swear, this is it, I'm not going to smoke anymore."

"How do you know? This is classic positive conditioning. You don't smoke, and you get no money. Then you smoke, and you get 10,000 euros. This will leave a good impression of smoking on you. You're cursed now!'

"And if you don't give me the money, you think I won't smoke?"

"So where do you want me to hand you the money? It's all in twenties, five hundred crisp fucking notes."

"I don't know. Just imagine how much money has changed hands in this hotel over the years. Millions and millions in all sorts of currencies. Can you imagine how many politicians and murderers have met here and handled cash?"

"Mostly dollars, I imagine."

The two men walked past the piano, past where the cross-legged beauty sat no more, down the marble stairs, into a men's room stall, where they counted out the money for a long while and farted sonorously when done.

Months have passed since the meeting in which Jovan received 10,000 euros, and he has spent all of it—productively—adding a room to his house, building a fish pond and a dove cote, and paying for his daughter's wedding. Nevertheless, when he thinks of the inheritance, he usually mutters, The only thing I got from my dead uncle was a smoking habit. He rolls his own cigarettes, as the commercial ones are too expensive, and smokes them like that, like a German student, and the smoke bites him and tastes acidic and stinging, and Jovan swears, *Jebem ti otadjbinu, Fuck the fatherland!* and smokes more.

Just today, Danko called him on the phone after the news of Milosevic's arrest. "I can't quit," he said, "can you?"

"No. I managed to quit for a day, but then when NATO bombed us, and they were hitting pretty close, as Batajnica has the largest military airport in the country, I bought a pack and smoked."

"How is Serbia now?"

"I've lost all sense of nationalism. I don't care for Serbia. NATO can bomb it again for all I care. So how do you make a living over there?"

"With the inherited money, I bought the junkyard on the western hill outside of Daruvar, so now I am a scrap-metal dealer, smashed cars, old Dalit factory machine parts. Nobody needs that old machinery, so it's all iron, steel, lead, aluminum, copper."

"Good for you. At least you are helping clean up a dismantled place. All our factories are gone, and we used to be a nation of proud workers."

"Oh, we used to be young, and when you're young, everything is good."

"I miss the nature in our hometown. The trees in the park must all be bigger now. I would love to see the trees again."

"Come back, then."

"I am often there in my thoughts. Whenever I smoke, I think of Daruvar. Smoke is the flavor of my memories."

"You sound nostalgic."

"Yes, positively sappy. And so I smoke. This burning sensation in me just keeps going and going. I enjoy feeling that I am ashes going to ashes."

ECLIPSE NEAR GOLGOTHA

After a scud missile from Iran missed habitations and hit a sandy rock near the Tomb of Joseph in Palestine, an emaciated Bedouin found old, parched paper in the sand. While herding goats, he used the scroll, not suspecting it was a Dead Sea Scroll, to roll cigarettes. Only a few triangular scraps of crumbly paper remained afterward, and we have very little to go by, but this conjectured story is the best that, after serious scholarship at Princeton and Oxford, could be pieced together. The poor Bedouin smoked away a lot of alternative wisdom about the past and the future into the desert air.

We can never rely on a singular interpretation in our world of parallel and perpendicular and elliptical views and visions. And on the cross, we apparently had parallel visions of a believer and a skeptic, and of the man in the middle, Jesus, who was both a believer and a skeptic, but his story has been covered enough. Let's first see what we find in Luke's gospel.

Chapter 23:39: One of the criminals who were hanged there was hurling abuse at Him, saying, Are You not the Christ? Save Yourself and us! *40* But the other answered, and, rebuking him, said, Do you not even fear God, since you are under the same sentence of condemnation? *41* And we indeed are suffering justly, for we are receiving what we deserve for our deeds; but this man has done nothing wrong. *42* And he was saying, Jesus, remember me when You come in Your kingdom! *43* And He said to him, Truly I say to you, today you shall be with Me in Paradise.

The nonbeliever wanted to be saved from the cross. He didn't mean to insult Jesus, but in the meager hope that Jesus was telling the truth, he appealed to Jesus to save him. And when it became clear that Jesus had no intention of surviving, let alone saving others, he shouted, Oh, the hell with it all! Jesus and the ingratiating thief had resigned themselves to death, and for a while the three of them kept groaning in pain. But the two believers died about the same time, and the remaining, the nonbeliever, by the name of Gestas, felt lonely and forsaken. It had been easier to suffer in the community of groaning which the three of them had made. Groaning alone and grinding his teeth, for he still had hale teeth, exasperated him so much that he shouted, Oh God, why have You forsaken me? Aren't we all Your children?

Two Roman foot soldiers, who had buried the other two convicts, came back and said, Look, this one is still shouting. What endurance!

Yes, some thieves are really tough, said the other. Nearly indestructible. This one was caught once after hiding in the desert for forty days without any food and water, and he escaped, but now we got him. There's no way he'll escape. Yes, he looks tough and indestructible.

We'll see about that, said a soldier, and threw his heavy lance into Gestas's side, nailing his body to the wood. Gestas shrieked and gasped and blood poured out of his wound, and soon also out of his nostrils, foamy and light red, translucent in the light of dawn. As soon as he was taken down, the sunshine dimmed, for there was an eclipse in progress, and in the strange, metallic gloom, the soldiers buried this bleeding man in a cave in the tomb garden outside the city walls near the Skull hill.

He was alone indeed, and moreover, clinically dead. There were no clinics around, and perhaps thus there were no clinical deaths in that era, but let's say he was clinically dead. Jesus and Dismas had already ascended to heaven, fulfilling Jesus's words, *For you shall be with me in paradise today already.*

Gestas suddenly believed all this, and he felt jealous, and prayed to God. Why has thou forsaken me? Dismas was a better thief than I; he stole gold, while I stole only sheep and goats, and I don't know anything about Jesus, except I heard he was a wine thief and he wanted to lead a revolution against the Romans and be the King of Israel, but let's say I am the worst. But is salvation the matter of being good? And of believing? So what if I don't believe in You, God. Why should I? You have been better to everyone than to me. Did I have to die so the other two could live? Did I die for them? Someone has to be dead and in the ground after the crucifixion, and so it's me. Oh, God, can I get some credit for this? I haven't lived enough. I haven't had any wine from the Golan yet. I haven't made any children. I haven't made love yet. Could I at least get to live three more days? And praying thusly, Gestas sank further into death.

In the meanwhile, outside, the eclipse passed and the sun warmed the rocks. It became extremely hot. At night, a hailstorm chilled the rocks, and thunder and lightning and an earthquake shook Heaven and Earth.

The rumbling of the earth cracked the rocks, and the stone blocking the entrance to Gestas's tomb rolled off. Moreover, all this rumbling and fresh cold air stirred Gestas. The cold air was God's breath blowing life into the pierced corpse. Gestas crawled out, and the sun blinded him and he didn't see anything for a while. He breathed deep, and crawled toward a murmuring sound nearby, where he washed his face and drank the tears of God, which flowed in a stream for the ways of our world had saddened the Lord God so.

And after drinking from this stream of sorrow, Gestas shook himself alive with the bitter and salty taste of universal sadness. And he awoke from his horrifying dreams and nightmares of being in Hell and consorting with Satan and smoking a variety of leaves with his hair on fire. Gestas now didn't know where to go, and sat in the cave, where the cool darkness cured his vision from too much light. He sat on a rock, which cut into his buttocks, looked back at the two little graves and an antechamber. He wondered whether the other two had been there before being whiffed up in a holy cloud straight into Heaven.

In the meanwhile, a young man saw him, and said, Jesus? Is that You?

Gestas didn't know how to reply. He was dazed, and didn't know whether he indeed was alive, whether he was himself. And he said, Yes, maybe it's Me.

Soon, the disciples came, and Peter kissed the son of man, and said, You are the son of God indeed!

And Thomas said, He looks a little different. His beard is much longer than Jesus's and he's taller.

You can feel the hole where the lance went in, said Gestas, and you can also feel the hole in My back, where the lance tip exited Me.

And Thomas did so, and said, Yes, this is Jesus.

And Simon said, Beards grow faster in death, and when you are thinner you look longer. This indeed is Jesus.

And Gestas found all this amusing, and smiled and asked, Where are My sisters? And where is wine? For we shall celebrate life and thank the Lord for His kindness.

And there ensued a big festivity, in which Gestas experienced the things he had missed in his busy life of stealing and grilling sheep and hiding in the desert and eating grasshoppers when there were no sheep. And Mary Magdalene washed him in aromatic oils, and Gestas was happy, and said, It's good to be Jesus.

One could say that this was identity theft, and if so, who should be better at it than a stealer of sheep? And it would not be the first identity theft—for hadn't Jacob stolen Esau's hairy identity by putting goatskin over his arm to obtain the blessing of blind Isaac? So if Gestas had pulled wool over the disciples' eyes, and passed himself for Jesus, he carried on the tradition to obtain the blessings of his followers. Three women armed with aromatic oils oiled him and anointed him the way David had been anointed.

Unfortunately, the Bedouin, who died during an Israeli raid of the Gaza strip while he was in a hospital, had smoked too much of the Dead Sea Scroll for us to know more about how the frolic with disciples and a variety of Marys and Marthas and Leahs went, whether Gestas indeed had the wish fulfilled to create a son of his own, or whether he died childless, and whether he evaporated from Mt. Moriah like Mohammed 599 years later, or whether he whiffed into stardust from the Ascension hill or the future Ammunition hill, and whether the grateful and ingratiating thief had done the same with Jesus. We know very little thanks to the infernal fires of tobacco, but with a few sips of red wine from the Golan Heights, we might yet be able to piece the story together, with a great deal of imagination and faith.

WANDERER

Neda, a blue-eyed fourteen-year-old with a swinging black ponytail, was walking down Brothers Wolf Street in Vinkovci and posting black-and-white photocopies of a longhaired Persian cat. There was no need for many colors, as the cat was white and would be so in a color photo as well. The cat evinced a pensive, perhaps angry or mistrustful expression, so that if a passerby read the text—*A three-year-old female cat, lost. If you find Mimi, call...*—he might think she had deliberately run away. And that is what a middle-aged man said, startling Neda, in English. "Are you sure Mimi hasn't simply run away?"

She stared at the man's thick, curly beard, his long salt-and-pepper hair, and the crow's feet around his hazel eyes.

"Pretty cat," he said.

"I ran out of tacks."

"No problem!" The stranger stuck the paper to the red bark of the fir tree by its resin. The tree could have been a good Christmas tree in its youth but was now shaggy, its branches drying out, and it bore scars of shrapnel from the war a quarter century ago. The scars kept bleeding resin and failed to heal.

"Are you a refugee?" she asked him. "I've read a lot about refugees, but I haven't seen one yet. You look Syrian."

"You could say that."

"Why aren't you in a group?"

"Maybe, like your cat, I left a group."

"How did you get here?"

"Across the Danube and through the cornfields."

"But there were warnings that the fields could be mined."

"Of course, just to scare people away. How would you grow corn in a minefield?"

"Where are you from?"

The man rolled his eyes. They were large and clear. "Wait a minute," he said, "I see her!" Just then, the white cat meowed from the top of the weeping fir tree. "See, she's not lost, she's treed! She doesn't know how to get down, and maybe she doesn't want to."

The stranger climbed the tree swiftly. Some of the thinner branches cracked as he stepped on them, but he didn't lose his grip. Neda feared that the tree would split. The stranger gripped the cat by the scruff of her neck and climbed down. He didn't look where his feet went, but they seemed to have an intelligence of their own. Even the little stubs of branches supported him, despite his weight.

When the man landed on the grass, Mimi hissed, as though not recognizing Neda. She grasped the cat and cried for joy, kissing its ears.

"Thank you so much," she said to the stranger.

"Oh, nothing to thank me for."

"Are you thirsty?" she asked, noticing his chapped lips.

"I can't deny that."

"Well, come home with me and I will give you a glass of water."

When they came home, she shouted, "Mom, we found Mimi!"

Mom, a lean redhead dressed in a plaid miniskirt, came out and saw the stranger. "And who is this? What are you doing here, sir?" she asked in Croatian.

"I don't think he understands Croatian, but you can talk to him in English."

"I am insecure in English. German, perhaps."

"He found the cat just as I was putting up the picture on a tree. And I invited him home because he's thirsty."

"How can you just pick up a stranger in the street like that? It's not safe to talk to older men. Most of them are perverts."

"I know that, but he's no stranger anymore. He's part of the family. He saved my cat."

"We are not supposed to just let them in. I should call the police to see whether he's properly registered. It's illegal to just take them in randomly."

The stranger drank water and said, "Thank you. Your kindness means a lot to me. And now, I am off."

"Where to?" asked Neda. "Not to Germany, I hope. What's so good in Germany? Why do you all want to go there?"

"No, not to Germany," he said. "I can't speak for all of them, but it's not for me. I am Jewish, and the history of that country and the lack of sunshine put me off."

"I thought you were Arabic."

"Arabic too."

"Mom, why don't we invite him to stay overnight? It's getting late."

"Oh, don't worry about me," the stranger said. He walked to the door and opened it. A strong wind blew and rattled the world, and it thundered, and a shower of hail beat down.

"Do wait at least till the rain is over," Neda said. "And you must be hungry by now."

"I cannot deny that."

"Here, we have some bratwurst," Mom said.

"I don't eat pork."

"Oh, look at him," Mom said. "He's starving but so finicky he won't eat pork. What next, he'll want gluten-free?"

"Well, Mom, they have religions like that, not to eat pigs. I'm glad we don't eat cats."

Mom brought out a jar of honey, some warm white bread, and milk. The stranger said, "Danke schön," and smiled, revealing his misaligned white teeth.

"How about some red wine," offered Mom. "Is that against your religion?"

"May I have a glass?"

The stranger poured water into his tall glass of ruby-red wine, Plavac Mali.

"You are diluting it," Mom said.

"No, this way there will be more." He drank, and kept pouring water into the glass, and the wine stayed ruby, refracting the light into swift arrows. The stranger sighed with relief and satisfaction, and while sitting in the red living room armchair he fell asleep.

They arranged the sofa with a pillow and a down cover and guided the stranger to it. He snored.

Marko, Neda's bald father, showed up around ten in the evening, smelling of cigarettes and brandy. "Who is this alcoholic bum sleeping on our sofa?"

Neda was still up, posting pictures of Mimi on Facebook. "Dad, he's not a bum. He found my cat! I love my cat, and I love the stranger because he saved Mimi."

"But he reeks of wine and sweat. I thought Muslims didn't drink wine. What kind of refugee is he?"

"Well, don't you think you'd want a glass of wine after a hard journey like that? I wonder whether he took a boat from Turkey to Greece. Haven't you heard that so far six hundred people have drowned crossing from Turkey to Greece?"

"Yeah, what's up with these boats. Can't these bums walk on the water? Maybe they don't have enough faith, fuck them. And there's land connecting Turkey and Greece. There are bridges, aren't there? If they want to go to Germany, and the Germans want them, why don't Germans just send a bunch of airplanes down there and take them? Who needs them here? Anyway, he's just a bum, you can see that, he's unwashed and he drinks. I hate drunks."

"He's not Muslim but Jewish. And I am sure he'd love a bath. Turn the boiler on?"

"That's ridiculous, there are no Jewish refugees."

"I don't think he's a refugee, but a wandering Jew," Neda said. "But really, isn't being a refugee like the main thing in Judaism? They left Egypt and wandered for forty years."

"Yeah, a great sense of direction, just look at the map, it's not such a great distance."

"Maybe that's why the Israelis developed GPS," Neda said.

"For a young brat, you have lots of information. Where do you get shit like that?"

"I read *Jutarnji* online."

Meanwhile, the stranger woke up, rubbed his eyes, and began to recite the Lord's Prayer in Aramaic.

Marko walked out to smoke and came back. "The damned hail wrecked the new cement on the balcony. I'll have to do it again. And moreover, I didn't get paid this month. The construction company is broke. Nobody builds anything here anymore. We only know how to destroy. And we aren't all that good at it, either." He sat down, sighed, and smoked more, coughed.

He ate three pale penises of bratwurst and drank Šljivovica, plum brandy, and smoked more. He stood up and walked to the larder and took out a slab of bacon, and with a sharp knife sliced away the thick bottom skin and tossed it out the window for the dog, who growled with gratitude. Then he gave a thin slice to Mimi, who sniffed at it, walked around the slice, and tried to bury it with dust from the floor.

"Oh, you little bitch," shouted Marko. "You are too fine for this? You think it's shit? It may be shit, but it's good shit."

Marko kicked the cat, and Neda shouted, "You asshole, how dare you!"

"Don't talk to your father like that!"

"Or what, you'll kick me and beat me, to teach me not to trust men?"

"It's not pop psychology, you brat. You just can't talk like that!"

"Leave my cat alone!" Neda crawled to the cupboard whispering, "Mitzzz, mitzz," but Mimi hissed and spat and growled from the narrow space between the tiled floor and the plywood of the furniture, perhaps saying in her language, *I've had enough of this shit, I am going back to my tree, next time don't bother to look for me. I'll eat sparrows and mice, and that will be better than the crap you feed me.*

Marko picked up the bit of bacon and threw it out the window to the dog, the furry devil, who welcomed the tidbit with a snap of his jaws.

Marko laid out the bacon on the cutting board and sliced and ate it raw, and chewed with his jaw clanking loudly. "You disgusting pig," his wife said.

"Oh, lovely to hear your voice," he said. "And what pig are you talking to? It's dead and not disgusting! And what is this? In this family, only the dog likes me."

The stranger had stopped whispering in Aramaic. Marko offered him bacon, and Mom said, "Do we have to explain again that it's against his religion?"

"And what is his religion?"

"*Ich bedauere, dass ich Englische besser nicht spreche,*" Mom said to the stranger.

"*Oh, dass ist alles in Ordnung,*" replied the stranger.

"*Warum sprechen Sie Deutsch? Wo haben Sie die Sprache gelernt?*" asked Marko.

"It's easy for me. It's basically Yiddish."

"You grew up among the Jews?"

"So I did."

"Who is your father?"

"I have no idea. My mother says he disappeared in the Six-Day War, and he left her pregnant with me before she got a chance to find out who he was."

"So where did you grow up?"

"In East Jerusalem, near Herod's Gate."

"And how did you join this band of refugees?"

"Who says I joined anything? Neither a follower nor a leader be! By the way, do you mind if I have another glass of wine?"

"Not at all."

The stranger drank half of it, topping it off with water.

"You behave like a regular Dalmatian," said Marko. And he kept slicing bacon and chewing it, while the stranger drank wine contemplatively.

Marko drank more Šljivovica, stepped out to smoke, came back, chewed more bacon with white bread, grew red in the face, gasped, and fell off the chair, which splintered into pieces. He made croaking sounds on the floor.

"My God," shouted Mom. "He's having a heart attack!"

"Do something!" shouted Neda. But neither she nor Mom could move, shocked by the sight.

Pretty soon Marko stopped moving, probably dead. Foam appeared in his nostrils, reddish. A breath came out of him, like the last air of a flat tire, and he grew still.

"Call an ambulance, for God's sake," said Neda.

Mom shouted, "Oh my God, my God!"

"Yes?" answered the stranger. His lips were red from wine, all the cracks of skin healed by the redness.

"Yes, what?" Mom said.

"God is a good idea," said the stranger, "especially now. You don't need an ambulance, there's not enough time. By the way, sometimes I talk to the Heavenly Father. You may think I am crazy, that I suffer from the Jerusalem syndrome, as many visitors of our beautiful city do. I think the Father will help us here."

He kneeled on the ground, turned Marko onto his back, and pumped his chest with his palms. Then he leaned over and did CPR for a minute.

Marko groaned, inhaled deeply, coughed, and sat up. "What happened?" he asked, and stood up with the stranger's assistance.

"You've had yourself a little heart attack. But you'll be all right, old sport," said the stranger, and gave Marko a slap on the shoulder. "I think you are better off drinking red wine," he said, and poured more of it. "Maybe that's how you'll remember me when I am gone."

Mom said, "How did you manage that? Are you a doctor? A Jewish doctor? I heard they were good."

They kept drinking all night long, listening to the stranger's stories, fell asleep, and when they woke up, they remembered not a single word of these stories, and both the stranger and Mimi were gone, not a trace of them. Neda found Mimi on Brothers Wolf Street, atop the weeping Christmas tree, which had shed even more resin tears overnight for the sorry world, so that Neda's jeans got all sticky climbing it. As for where the wandering Jew was, Mimi couldn't offer an answer in a language Croats would understand.

IDEAL GOALIE

Davor traveled from Frankfurt to Eindhoven by train. He was exhausted from the long hours of work on construction sites as a *Gastarbeiter*—a guest worker—from Croatia. He cursed himself for not studying more at school and not becoming a doctor. But how could he study? Soccer was everywhere, games were always on, and he played pick-up soccer with his friends. Despite Yugoslavia being a poor country that couldn't retain its players for very long before they all emigrated abroad, where they usually played better than they did at home, one of its clubs was in the final round of sixteen.

It was his favourite club, Hajduk. Davor blushed a little to think he'd collected signatures to vote the Hajduk goalie as the most handsome player in the league. He was eleven when he did that, and the Belgrade newspaper, *Tempo*, published the votes that he'd mailed in from his hometown, Omis, near Split. He had forged half of the votes, and Vukcevic came in third. Bjekovic from Partizan was first, but that simply had to do with the fact that Partizan had more fans than Hajduk. Now he laughed at himself for the childhood naiveté and the terrible waste of time.

He watched the plains while on the train. It rained, and the rain made the window look like old glass, distorting the soggy landscape of hops plantations and stuccoed houses, each one of which displayed a row of red or yellow aspidistras in the windows. He longed for his native rocky beaches and fig trees. Fresh figs, green on the outside but purple and brown on the inside, tasting heavenly, slippery, and sweet in the sun. Lizards crawling under the stones.

Outside his compartment sat a Kosovo man on a huge disk of cheese, which he must have brought along from home—his capital to deliver to a restaurant. It looked better and more reliable than currency, and was probably pretty comfortable to sit on. At the Dutch border, the man was ordered off the train, and the police interrogated him about his cheese. Because he had long hair, Davor was harassed at the border too, and even his toothpaste was squeezed out in search of illegal drugs.

"Why is it that the only two people ordered off the train are from Yugoslavia?" Davor asked in German.

"It's just a coincidence."

"Why don't you bother Germans and Englishmen?"

"We don't bother anybody, we are simply doing our job," was the reply.

Davor made it to Eindhoven and walked into a bar to fortify himself with some Grolsch before the game. He popped the patented beer cap and drank from the green glass.

At the stadium, he was surprised to see some of the old players on the Hajduk team: Jerkovic, Vukcevic, Holcer, along with some new ones such as Buljan, a tall, bony, thuggish player who could stop anyone and who could run through a defense in a straight line. Davor drank whiskey and shouted, "Hajduk, Hajduk, *samo naprijed!*" Forward, Outlaws!

A powerful wind blew away the Hajduk cap he'd had for years. Newspapers, umbrellas, flowers, they all flew across the stadium, carried by violent gusts. Davor felt a bit asthmatic. That damned cement dust was probably turning his lungs into a wall, and any change in the availability of oxygen affected him.

His idols ran out onto the field. What tall and powerful men! Raised in Split, in the sun, eating small fish with the bones, they'd grown up to be bony, strong, with an aura of vigor to them. Vukcevic came out last, and he was a bit pale and green-ish in the face, as though he wasn't feeling quite right. Davor imagined what must have been going on in the man's head—maybe Vukcevic had enjoyed himself too much the night before?

Vukcevic stood unsteadily in front of his goal. The night before, the team had stayed up a little too late, excited by the Dutch hospitality. He'd made love without a condom to a boisterous girl, and now he had an itch, and he wondered whether it came from too much rubbing or some disease. How will I go back to my wife? I'll have to use condoms at home if I don't abroad. Why did I do it? Sure it was nice, somehow very slippery, more so than at home.

The whole trip had thrilled Vukcevic. Just as he had imagined, the wind moved picturesque windmills in the country outside of Eindhoven, and lifted many miniskirts downtown. After taking a walk, he'd had a hard-on like an adolescent. The skirts shook in the wind like an invitation, and a girl on a bicycle chatted him up. "I've seen your picture," she said. "I hope you won't defend your goal too well."

She lifted one of her legs and planted the other on the pave-ment. Her thigh was long and graceful and it glistened.

"I hope you won't defend yours," he said.

"Mine, what?"

"Your...well."

"Is that like a proposition?"

"If you are going to answer yes, it is."

Now he wondered whether she had been sent by Dutch soc-cer fans, or even the club managers. A pretty good strategy—get the goalie wasted, keep him up all night, get him to smoke hash-ish and drink wine and beer, and then send him into the field.

He fought a gag reflex full of Grolsch fumes and burped, and the wind beat back his burp and filled him with air. He felt bloated and weak; the wind could pick him up and he'd fly out of the stadium like a balloon.

He stood some ten paces in front of the goal when, totally unpredictably, the wind carried the ball from a midfield kick from the opposing team and missed his net by a few feet. That would have been totally embarrassing if the Dutch had scored like that.

He kicked the ball out as hard as he could, high in the air, but the wind brought it back to him like a boomerang, and the Dutch, who seemed to understand playing in the wind, were all in Hajduk's half. A ball that didn't look like a hard kick acceler-ated and suddenly changed direction. Instead of his catching it with his hands, it hit him on the head and he fell to the ground. He stood up like a boxer after a knockout.

At one moment Buljan knocked down a player, who had passed nearly the entire Hajduk defense, in the penalty zone. An eleven-meter kick was assessed. That would certainly be a score for the Dutch. Vukcevic tried to read where the ball would go by the angle of the striker's feet. It looked like it would be a low shot to the right. Instead of flying to catch the ball, as he'd usually do, he stood in the same spot. The ball went straight at him and hit him in the chest, bounced, and he jumped forward and caught it as the Dutch player rushing the goal leapt to avoid hitting him.

The stadium burst into screams. It looked as though the goalie was brilliant for not letting himself be faked. Every goalie took a chance to fly based upon a read and, if a fake was even a bit decent, it was sometimes easiest to strike in the middle of the goal. Most experienced and self-confident penalty kickers occasionally chose to do that. Thanks to total inertia, he'd made a save.

That was that—now he couldn't ask to be replaced. The hard ball hitting his rib cage had knocked the air out of him, and he was even dizzier than before. Luckily, a couple of balls flew by him and the goal post, and it simply looked as though he was a good reader of shots.

Then there was another penalty kick. He had no time to move and the ball was in the net, in the very top corner. A minute later, another ball somehow landed in the net. He hadn't noticed how that had happened, but it clearly had. Still, it wasn't all that bad because Hajduk had scored as well.

It was the ninetieth minute. Hajduk had won 1-0 in Split, and if the score stayed 2-1 for Eindhoven PSV, Hajduk would go on because scoring on the opponent's turf counted for more than scoring at home. So, Hajduk had basically won. The players were kissing and hugging each other, and Vukcevic was biding the time, placing the ball on the sixteen-meter line to kick out, then changing his mind. He rolled the ball, put it down again, and picked it up. The referee warned him that the game would be extended if he kept it up.

Vukcevic tossed the ball and wanted to run at it but slipped and almost fell. His gag reflex came back. Had he indulged in oral sex as well? What would happen to his gums? It was the wrong moment to think about that. The referee extended the game for one more minute and gave Vukcevic a yellow card for avoiding active play.

He'd managed to burn at least twenty more seconds anyway, and if he kicked the ball far enough, into the jungle of players, everything would be all right. He tossed the ball in the air and kicked as hard as he could. The wind shifted the ball's trajectory, so that instead of kicking with the tip of his shoe, he connected with the roof of his foot. Nevertheless, it was a fine and strong kick and the ball went high up.

He had an incredible itch, and so he scratched his groin and didn't follow the path of the ball. When he lifted his gaze he was amazed to see that the ball was flying back above him. Another gust of the wind brought it down, right under the goal post.

The crowd exploded with jubilant screams. The Croatian players sank to their knees. The score was 3-1 for PSV. The goalie had scored against his own team, or more precisely the wind had, but since he was the last one to touch the ball, he was the human agent of self-destruction.

He apologized to his teammates, but none would talk to him. A long line of Dutch fans, mostly blonde women, awaited his autograph. Auto-goal was enough, he would not autograph. Their faces blurred in his mind, and they all looked like the woman from the night before. He tried to spit, but his mouth was dry.

Outside the stadium, as he walked to the bus, he heard Croatian *Gastarbeiter* screaming obscenities at him. Yes, it was terrible that he'd let them down like that. But he did save a penalty kick. Sure, these workers lived miserably abroad and wanted a little bit of joy. But was it his fault that they were such losers, that they had nothing else to live for? The world was a big place, full of opportunities, and if you couldn't find any other source of hope than a stupid game, you deserved no pity. Or you deserved pity, but wouldn't get any of his sympathy. He flashed the international go-fuck-yourself sign and turned his back on his compatriots.

Davor saw Vukcevic's fuck-you sign. After all those trips, hard-earned tickets, to see his idol behave so arrogantly!

Two weeks later, Davor took a night train to Split for a brief vacation, unpaid leave. He'd been drinking steadily since Haj-duk's loss. At one point, he'd twisted his ankle, and now it was swollen. He wrapped it up in a shirt, which he kept soaking in cold and salty water. Once he got home and soaked the foot in the Adriatic, he would recover fast, his foot anyway, but he would still grieve for his soccer club, and even more for all those years he had followed soccer, eagerly awaiting games, listening to the radio, and all those mornings and evenings he spent discuss-ing the previous night's soccer match with his friends, and the games yet to be played. He had remembered all the games, all the moves, all the players…what a waste! Who would compen-sate him for all that garbage in his head? He could have learned the names of all the trees and medicinal plants and mushrooms, and even all the fucking stars in the heavens, but now he had a headful of soccer stats. In a few years, nobody would remember these arrogant boys who had made the nation breathless, ner-vous, always awaiting victories that rarely transpired. There is no greater unhappiness than that of a fan of a relatively good, extremely talented club that somehow never makes it.

He was in a compartment with a German tourist going on vacation. When she leaned down to remove her water bottle from her backpack, her breasts swayed, unfettered by a bra. The train conductor came and made love to the tourist. Davor pre-tended to sleep but the noises made him too excited.

When the conductor left, the tourist still lay there with her skirt pulled up.

Davor came over and touched her knee.

She slapped him, hard.

"What's that for?" he asked. "Don't you want to do it?"

"Get lost or else."

He was ashamed. How come she wanted the train conductor and not him? Maybe they'd had a soulful conversation, maybe the conductor forgave her a fare, and what could Davor offer her? Neither soul nor fare. He went back to his side of the compartment and stretched out. He couldn't sleep all night.

In the morning, in Split, he drank some coffee in the first café he could find along the walls of the Diocletian Palace. He certainly didn't miss the flavour, but nevertheless he drank the espresso that must have come from the dregs, a second or third run through the same grind. Suddenly he noticed Vukcevic several tables away, drinking with a beautiful brunette in a white tennis dress, probably a model. So, you bastard, he thought, you can still be happy. You give us heart attacks when we watch your games, and here you are, relaxing, happy, adored.

He even had the gall to emanate charisma. He looked very well, somewhat plump, his black hair shining, with strong eyebrows and a twinkle in his eyes, as though he'd just come up with a clever joke, and he probably had.

Davor noticed there was a souvenir shop, and he walked over to it. He bought a hunting knife with the Hajduk circle-of-wheat emblem engraved in the imitation ivory handle, and then jauntily strolled toward Vukcevic. He visualized lifting the knife and shouting, "For Eindhoven!" The knife hit the shoulder blade and went through it, partly, but stopped. Davor left the knife stick-

ing in the bone and turned to run. He'd forgotten about his
ankle. It twisted again, turning outward, and he fell.

The part here that was not imagined was that he fell with
the knife in his hand just as he was shouting "For Eindhoven,"
but the knife was still in his hand, and clearly he hadn't stabbed
Vukcevic, although he did have a momentary blackout during
his fall. He wasn't sure whether it was before the fall or after
that his mind blanked out.

A couple of young men got to him and lifted him to his feet.

"You wanted to stab Vucko?"

"He lost the game for us."

"Come on, you can't take it that seriously. You can't go killing the players now! We're taking you to the police station."

But three other guys came by and said, "Let him go! He had
the right idea. We should go and get them all, those lazy motherfuckers. Give me that knife, I'll stab the bum!"

A brawl ensued, and pretty soon there were several dozen
people fighting. Davor looked down the block and saw Vukcevic
running away. He wished he could see a knife sticking out of the
man's back, with red streaks of blood running down the white
shirt, but there was only a bright white shirt, glaring in the sun,
beyond the several dozen young men who fought over whether
or not to kill the players. They were so absorbed in their fight
that they ignored Davor, who limped to the train station.

STRINGS

On Columbus and 106th, opposite a hotel on whose yellow neon sign a green monkey leaped and hung by its tail during the summer, near a burnt-down cancer ward, I shared an apartment with three Juilliard students. At first, there were five of us. My ex-Soviet roommate's brother was one. The two ex-Soviets, fresh from the exile camp in Vienna, spoke no English and didn't dare to leave the apartment. They spent the whole summer on a floor mattress, wrapped in a white sheet, embracing, gazing at a small TV we had found in a garbage heap on the Upper East Side. The antennae, sticking out like a V sign, could catch only one channel, which trembled and shifted up and down. When summer was over, the ex-Soviets stood up from the bed, speaking fluent English. The brother moved out and opened an ESP therapeutic center in Chinatown.

A French violinist slept on the floor in an Alpine sleeping bag. Whenever he woke up, he rubbed his sweaty and hairy chest with a thick towel, and his bloodshot eyes stared at us as though we were the Andean cannibals, cooking him for supper. We had no air conditioning. On hot days, he woke up in puddles of his own sweat.

I slept on the carpet from a rich man's garbage heap. The only one of us who had a real bed was a Swiss cellist, who shaved twice a day and resentfully looked around him at the chaos the rest of us created with our clothes, papers, bread crumbs, utensils, shoeshine boxes, records, toothpaste tubes. I easily got used to the bohemian atmosphere, and paid no thoughts to how different it all was from what I had expected of my stay in America.

But as my roommates and I ran through our apartment after a rat, stumbling over ashtrays, beer cans, unwashed plates with dry and cracked yolks, it occurred to me: Is this the way to live? Where are the cats?

I didn't wish to chase the rodent; he looked like a veteran of many battles, and that he was in the predicament of having a crew of Juilliard musicians after him was no doubt a result of his observing us for a while and correctly assessing us to be a bunch of wimps. He used to enter the kitchen at noon, charge the trash bag like a small boar, biting straight through the olive plastic in search of cheese crusts. We bought gourmet cheeses—since we snorted no coke, we had to have some wasteful recompense—which tasted the way cow dung, horse shit, a pigsty, and freshly cut grass smelled: strange how you grow to like the foul taste, but the fouler the tastier. The Frenchman scoffed at us for liking the cheeses, which, according to him, were bland. The stench of cheese must have thrown our rat back to his rural roots.

In the rat's first appearances, it was enough to set your foot in the kitchen, and he'd scurry off, squealing for his life. But after he had heard us playing Schubert string quartets, his caution vanished. Now he languidly rummaged through our garbage, looking fat and well established, and with an air of dignity, he strolled into the living room for the afternoon intermezzo.

Schubert moved him. I read somewhere that Bach moves plants. Schubert rooted our rat to the spot, making him tremble to the harmonics of minor keys, raising his hairs so that he resembled a hedgehog. Now and then he stood on his hind legs, put his paws together like a squirrel praying for a pistachio. Perhaps he would have clapped his paws, but didn't dare out of piety for the music. *Der Tod und das Mädchen* was his absolute favorite. We used to play it sometimes just to tease him. Then he'd come quite close to the cello; his little beady eyes shone with tears, his upper lips twitched, his little incisors pinching his lower lip.

If he hadn't been so scrawny, his ears so small, his tail so thin and wet, he could have passed for a squirrel and would have been quite likable. But Lord knows, he was not likable. Perhaps he wished to be. Perhaps he wished to make friends with us, and would have been proud of us. Perhaps he was proud of us. He may even have loved us. But we didn't appreciate him as the audience—after all, playing to entertain a rat is not what you'd call lustrous. Yet his listening always humored us and put a joie de vivre, otherwise so hard to come by, into the strings.

Still, we had to put a stop to his growing more and more brazen. Soon he would have been jumping on the table and dining with us. He would have grown so attached to us that he would have followed us on our dates, and certainly he would have been unstoppable if he had known Schubert's *Unfinished Symphony* would caress the walls at Avery Fisher Hall, though I should think he'd have preferred it at Carnegie, where walls, old and sandy, must be easier to bite through.

We discovered that he feared Bartók. I don't know why he feared Bartók; maybe he hadn't been educated well enough to take the stresses of modernity in music, though he kept up with other modernities and post-modernities as an NYC rat. Though Bartók made him run helter-skelter for shelter, we couldn't keep playing Bartók just to keep a rat away.

Alone, none of us could have handled the little Ayatollah. But united—a Frenchman, a Yugoslav, an ex-Soviet, and a Swiss— we dared to take him on. Actually, the Frenchman was away on a date with a woman from the fourth floor. He preferred a woman from the second floor, but one floor of elevator time was not enough for him to let her pick him up—that's how he described it. Three floors of elevator time sufficed for a woman to pick him up. So the three of us intervened, like United Nations Blue Helmets of sorts—and if the Swedish anticommunist and anti-feminist elite had given us a Nobel Prize for peace, we could have done even better.

As the rat strolled into our bathroom, we exchanged conspiratorial looks. It was too much; now he would like to share our toilet! The ex-Soviet jumped up and shut the bathroom door, swearing in Russian. The Swiss and I grabbed the table, the plates sliding and crashing on the floor. We barred the bathroom door. Then we opened it. Over the edge of the table, we aimed blows at the rat with a broomstick, a baseball bat (through which we had tried to Americanize ourselves), and an unscrewed table leg.

Only two of us could fit in the doorframe at a time, so we took turns. Mostly we missed. The Swiss struck him first with the broomstick, despite its being thin—Swiss precision, I guess, but let's stay away from stereotypes. The blow surprised the rat and incensed him. He shrieked gorily and jumped toward us, nearly the full height of the fence. I got goose bumps from the shrillness of his voice. We were almost ready to beat a retreat and sign a peace treaty, in Geneva if need be. But we were too ashamed.

The rat jumped again, right up to the edge of the table. As he was falling down, I struck him with the baseball bat, which brushed his back and squashed his tail on a tile. The tile broke in half. Hardly a second later, the table leg struck him, blowing him off the floor; his body hit the heating pipe. Now he jumped without any order, like a panicky frog, in such high leaps that he could have jumped over the table. He jumped left, and right, and then backward. He fell into the bathtub. He couldn't jump out of the slippery tub. We flung the table aside, the Swiss squealed *Ya'ohl*, and we all jumped forward. Blood squirted. The enamel of the tub cracked in many places.

When he was finally dead, instead of triumphant, we were ashamed; we didn't look into each other's eyes. Slowly we swept his remains onto a Sunday *New York Times Magazine* and put it into three olive garbage bags. We threw the package into a large rusty iron dumpster in a somber, funereal mood. We washed the tub for days with all sorts of soaps, until it shone. We threw away the clubs; henceforth, our table had only three legs. None of us took baths anymore, only showers, which of their own accord changed from hot to cold to hot.

If we had hoped that after the assassination we would be rat-free, we were wrong. A chap similar to our murdered friend began to appear—so similar that it spooked us. But he didn't care for music. We bought rat poison and put it in cheese. Either it didn't kill him or another rat, indistinguishable, replaced him. At night there were constant noises coming from the walls: scuffling of rats in their love, work (tunnel and road construction), and debates in muffled squeals.

One night a fire alarm went off. We didn't bother to get out of our beds; the alarm went off so often that it always seemed a prank. But when hollering reached our ears and smoke our nostrils, we looked out the window. Pointed blue and orange tongues of fire licked the walls above windows like tongues rolling over upper lips after a greasy meal. We grabbed our passports, diplomas, money, and instruments, leaving behind pictures of families and girlfriends, suits, records, music scores. In long underwear, we ran down the smoky stairs out of the building, into the slushy snow. Rats leaped out the windows and thumped against the pavement and scurried away.

Waiting, I got such a frostbite on my large toe that for a while it seemed it would have to be cut off, and probably would have been if I'd had a good enough insurance policy to visit a doctor. I still can't feel anything in the toe.

An orange school bus took us to shelter, and some shelter it was! People sick beyond repair, derelicts, drunks, drug addicts, lunatics, failed thieves who were still trying. We ran out of the stench and spent the night all rolled up in a bundle on a grating in a stream of urinated heat.

Several days later, the Frenchman, the ex-Soviet, and I moved back into our apartment. The Swiss cellist moved back to Switzerland. Although the building was now all sooty, the windows gaping black, our part was nearly intact. There were no rats, not for a year, when we filed a claim against our landlord in a small claims court, demanding to be paid back several months of rent because there had been no hot water and heat. Although the landlord didn't show up in the court, he won the case and evicted us.

REMOTE LOVE

Sirloin steak was served. The host had his done medium rare, his wife medium, and Tesla well. Tesla glanced at the hostess's luminous hair, with curls like copper coils.

When Tesla lifted his steak knife, it glistened like a mirror, elongating his face. Nevertheless, he rubbed the blade on several napkins while the hostess, Miriam, laughed at him. "What's the matter, Nikola? You think we're *filthy* rich."

"No, ma'am, you're as clean as they come, but we live in a filthy world. I have only used sixteen napkins here, while at the Waldorf Astoria I use seventeen. That shows you how much I trust you."

"You are insufferable! I don't know why we put up with you," she said.

"Oh, we know why we do," said the host, Sebastian, straightening his pointed silvery moustache.

Tesla scrutinized the wine in his glass for a few seconds, brought the glass to his thin lips, sipped, and swished the wine back and forth from one cheek to the other, enjoying the tart tightening of his gums. He sliced his steak into little cubes. He calculated the volume of each one before putting it into his mouth. He didn't need a ruler; his sense of proportion, he was sure, would precisely give him the lengths. The first cubic morsel was probably ~0.8888 cubic centimeters, loosely speaking. As long as it was smaller than one, he was pleased with the quantity. He was impressed that the numeral eight emerged, and he decided he would enjoy the dinner as a thematic variation on the number eight; he squared it into sixty-four and chewed patiently, counting to sixty-four.

Miriam observed his serrated jaw muscles working like an accordion. "My God, you are a patient eater."

"What is there to be impatient about?" he said. "It will take my stomach at least twenty-four hours to digest the beef. Why should it take my mouth less than sixty-four seconds to chew it?"

He looked into the hostess's eyes and, in the dim light, her pupils occupied more area than her blue irises—eight millimeters in diameter, which is to say, four in radius. Four squared times half of Pi. Of course, with each shift in the quantity of light, the diameter would change and so would the area. He carved an octagonal shape out of his steak. That's partly why he liked his steak well done, and why he liked the knives to be extremely sharp—so he could cut out regular shapes.

"Why, Nikola, you're a sculptor with your steak," Miriam said and glanced toward her husband, who was chewing obliviously with his eyes half closed to better concentrate on the joys of rare flesh. "It gives me pleasure to observe how precisely you cut it. Do you do everything so precisely?"

"No, ma'am. Many things can't be done precisely."

"Are you so precise in love as well?"

"Depends on what you mean by love. If you mean a wireless transfer of electricity, then, yes, of course—I will be very soon. First I need to raise the means for doing so."

"Oh, I don't mean that! That doesn't sound like love but physics." Miriam finished her second glass of Bordeaux.

Nikola Tesla had the sensation that she was gently rubbing the calf of his leg with her foot. He blushed and wasn't sure to what extent the flush in his cheeks was a result of the embarrassingly intimate bodily contact and how much of it was the dry wine and, at that moment, he had no idea how to establish a formula for solving the problem.

When Miriam stood up to visit the toilet, he still had the feeling of her foot rubbing his calf. An electrifying sensation crawled up his skin and into his scalp, similar to what he felt during the public demonstrations in which he conducted two million volts of electricity over the surface of his body. After the experiments, he would glow in the dark for a few seconds, all his hairs standing, magnetized, and his mind nearly swooning in electrical ecstasy. The hairs that protruded outside his cuffed and sharply starched white shirt, on the back of his palm, stood up. This reminded him of his old tomcat from his childhood. Having seen sparks of static before petting the cat in the dark, Nikola had asked his mother whether the world was one huge tomcat, with lightning all over it. Now he lifted the edge of the embroidered tablecloth to peer down and noticed that the outer calf of his leg was leaning against the wooden leg of the table.

He thought that his sensual reaction to the imaginary carnal contact with the hostess was treacherous of him, considering that his host, Sebastian Chesterfield, kindly invited him several times a month for dinner and, even more kindly, had bought some shares in the Nikola Tesla Company. And at the moment, Sebastian was speaking at the end of the table.

"We live in most peculiarly volatile times. It seems we could become the perfect society, but it's more likely that we will all end up in flames. These are sad days indeed."

"I think there has never been so much humour in the air," Nikola responded.

"How do you define humour?" Sebastian asked. "In the Greek way?"

"No, as in joking. For example, *Why does a policeman move to a corner whenever it gets cold in his room? Because he's heard that the corner is ninety degrees.*"

"For my part, I like the police," Sebastian commented.

Tesla gulped from his glass of water, despite seeing tiny particles hovering in it—bacteria or dust? He was afraid only of living organisms. His office was full of lead, asbestos, and all sorts of heavy metals and their dusts, and none of them did any harm to him. He washed the water down with wine and continued.

"*One afternoon, a Dalmatian man woke up with a shriek of horror. What's the matter? his brother asked. I had a dream that I was working.*"

"Sad, sad. It reminds me of how we indeed live in a world full of indolence," Mr. Chesterfield said.

"And how about this one? *Two Montenegrins stand on a dock and enjoy the sunset colors. One says to the other, Look, there's a man drowning! Oh, I see. And we are just standing. You're right. Let's sit down.*"

"You come up with so many patents," Miriam said, "it must be easy for you to come up with jokes."

"I dine with Mr. Clemens as often as I can in order to enjoy his witty conversation, but I can't come up with a joke. I'm pretty gloomy when left to my own devices, and I don't think humourously."

"Well, how about marriage?" asked Sebastian.

"You mean, if I really want to be gloomy?"

"He's an eligible bachelor, now, isn't he?" Sebastian addressed Miriam.

"Oh yes, so tall and dashing, with all these pending and pendulous patents." She swallowed a big gulp of wine, and the red lingered beyond the edge of her upper lip, on the superfine fuzz. "You need a business-savvy woman who will make sure you don't get cheated out of your proper royalties. Ann Morgan adores you. With her father's money, you'd never have to worry about financing your experiments."

"But she wears earrings," Tesla protested.

"She could take them off, if you told her to," Miriam said.

"But she would be offended."

"What's wrong with earrings?" she asked.

"The coiled metal so close to your brain interferes with your brain waves. You're not in full possession of your senses. It's quite possible that an advanced civilization from outer space could control you through high-frequency ether waves. I think it's enough to take a look at our fellow citizens to realize that many of them aren't real human beings but robots, controlled through their love of jewelry."

"Maybe you could control Ann's brain using your electro-magnetic toys," Sebastian suggested. "She could be your robot."

"You have a point. I better start working on a mechanism to harness an heiress's brain. I might change my attitude toward coiled bodily metals yet. But for now, I don't want to deal with Ann's jewelry."

"Rumor has it," said Sebastian, "that you could have become the richest man on earth if you hadn't torn up a contract for AC generators with Westinghouse."

"True. Westinghouse faced pressure from his investors to re-duce the amount and rewrite the contract—I thought he was my friend, so I tore up the contract. All he aimed for, most likely, was for me to reduce the amount in half. Even at fifty cents a kilowatt hour, I'd be the first billionaire on the continent."

"But then you wouldn't dine with us, would you?" said Miriam. "So there's a happy upshot to the story."

"I would dine with you, but we'd be doing it in my palace, illuminated by electricity directly from the far reaches of the universe."

"What a bastard, that Westinghouse," said Sebastian. "He could have protected you from your impulses."

"Well, he did give me a couple hundred thousand dollars, but I already spent all of that on my equipment and experiments."

"Amazing," Sebastian said. "How could you spend that much money in ten years?"

"My lab went up in flames a couple of times. Anyhow, I would have spent a hundredfold if I'd had it, but by now, we would live in a different world, without wires and rails. We would travel through air on electromagnetic waves, we'd talk to our European cousins on wireless telephones, we'd bomb our enemies with powerfully focused cosmic rays, with no need for guns and cannons."

A courier came running in. "A message from Wall Street. The markets are collapsing!"

Mr. Chesterfield stood up from the table. "Again? I'll be back in an hour."

"Do you need me to go with you?" asked his wife.

"I have to attend to this myself. You two just stay here, and I'll be back momentarily, when I see what shakes out. It's probably another false alarm."

The host swallowed the last bite of his bloody beef, which made his Adam's apple leap up and down like a valve, and he strode out of the room, his hard leather shoes drumming on the cherry-wood floors. Tesla felt the vibrations through the floor, and he had an impression that his shins were resonating with the floor's thudding.

Miriam leaned back in her chair, gathered her glowing hair behind her ears to reveal a strong jawline, and laughed merrily, her chest rising.

"What's funny?" asked Tesla.

"I'm happy even if you haven't invented a space vehicle yet."

The maitre d' came over and said, "How can I help you?"

"You can't. Go to your quarters and relax, that's how," she said.

The tall stooping man walked out gingerly without making a sound.

"Here your husband may be losing his fortune this very minute because the markets are collapsing, and you're happy."

"What do you care about the markets? They go up and down. And last time they went down, my husband bought up all sorts of stocks and tripled his wealth within a month when the markets rebounded."

"I could rejoice in the collapse of the financial world if it didn't mean my budget would be the first to go. Even my stock might be sinking."

"Oh, don't talk about stocks and become a bore like the rest of them. Let me show you a painting. It's in the library."

He followed her to the darkened brown room, where everything seemed to be hushed and subdued in tone except for a pale-skinned beauty by Ingres.

"Lovely forms, what clarity of skin," Tesla said. "But the visual arts are of no interest to me since I recall everything in full detail. I nearly flunked out of elementary school because I refused to draw. I didn't see why I should draw anything when I could totally recall it."

"How about your engine designs?"

"I don't need to draw them, except to explain to engineers what I mean. This is marvelous. Is that you? She looks just like you."

"How would you know what I look like? You can't see through my clothes, now, can you?"

"You could have posed for one of your famous artist friends. For this Ingres, for example."

There was a radiance and shine on her, but that may have simply been the result of a streak of light falling through an opening between the crimson velvet curtains and hitting her coiled hair. He wondered whether red hair contained more iron than hair of other colors. There was a powerful magnetic field around her, no doubt about that.

"Kiss me," Miriam said. Her mouth was half open, her moist lips glistening.

Tesla was tempted to lean over and kiss her, but he thought of just how many different kinds of bacteria and how many millions of them would be exchanged in a single kiss, and he shivered from fear. Each cubic milliliter exchanged could mean some incurable and as-yet-undiagnosed disease. Tesla had grown up surrounded by TB, malaria, pneumonia, and he did not want to sink into disease again. Sure, the disease could remind him of his native region, his village in Gorski Kotar. Getting a swallow of bacteria-rich saliva would be like manna from the homeland, something to cure him of nostalgia. Tesla was over six feet tall and so, to avoid the kiss, he simply straightened up. "I wish I was a painter and you posed for me."

"So you'd stand away. You wouldn't have to touch me, is that it? All right, as you wish."

She took a few steps back and threw her clothes off, her dress, her bodice, revealing a sensationally curvaceous body with her tilted hips. Tesla stretched out his arm and his fingertips reached toward her. He let his fingers come to within eight millimeters of her skin. She lay down on an ornate divan. He sensed her electromagnetic field exerting a pulling force to the iron in his blood, like a magnet, and the iron in his blood, once stirred, created magnetic waves that clashed with hers and stroked hers. He traced her body's shape over her skin without touching her. If he clashed with the lines of her magnetic field in a regular and harmonic manner, he could create electricity in her; and as she shifted she became the rotor of a human alternating-current generator. Her hairs stood up and she moaned. Sparks flew between his fingers and her skin, crackling and flashing. In the blue light of static, her skin appeared ephemeral and translucent.

After a certain amount of such remote stroking, he excused himself and went to the bathroom. He nearly swooned from the discharge he felt while leaning against the cold red marble tiles. He washed his hands with a new soap for several minutes, until he saw that his skin was creasing up.

He walked back and Miriam, who was flushed and breathless, was already dressed. Her hair was disheveled, and it occupied twice the volume it used to.

Tesla straightened his stiff collar. On his way out, on the white marble staircase, he ran into Mr. Chesterfield, who said, "False alarm. The market dipped but didn't collapse. Stay! Let's celebrate with the finest Italian wines."

"I can't celebrate now. Too much work to do."

"What are you working on?"

"The end of the world."

———

The following Tuesday, he didn't go to see the Chesterfields. It would be awkward to look Sebastian in the eye. Not that he would need to look him in the eye, or that he ever did really, but just knowing that he would have to avoid his eyes, that would be awkward. On the other hand, what did he do wrong? Did he make love with his wife? Perhaps he did, but he did not have sex with her, not in the graphic way anyhow. Or he had metaphysical sex; well, perhaps physical but not chemical. If there was a bio-chemical side effect, it was totally separate from hers; they didn't mingle their bodily contents. Still, he was distracted. As soon as he closed his eyes, even fleetingly, the image of red coppery coils glowed, filling his head with light. He wished he'd never looked into the curls, for they befuddled his mind. He would fight this, however, through the new project.

In his lab atop 64 East Houston Street, he worked on perfecting an oscillator that, when connected to a solid iron surface, could create waves of ever-increasing intensity. The light, synchronized taps of the iron rod would add to the wave, keep it growing and growing until it became a tremendous power that could destroy buildings. With a fist-sized oscillator, it would take him less than an hour to drop the Brooklyn Bridge into the East River.

Tesla worked for twenty hours each day and slept only for four, before dawn. The next Wednesday morning, while Tesla sipped rose hip tea, the mailman brought him a bundle of letters; one was from Miriam.

"You didn't make it to our dinner party yet again. Just when I thought we had attained a new level of friendship, you have begun to avoid us. Are you all right? How is your health? You have been looking very thin lately, so maybe it's not us, not me, you are avoiding. Do please let me know lest I should have to check on you in person."

Tesla finished the tea. While he tried to imagine energy waves, he visualized them alternately as the line from her pelvis ascending over the hips and waist and then as elliptical circling around her breasts, a numeral 8 laid down, a blue wave traveling atop one breast, then below another and back. In size, he wondered what the proportion of the breast wave was to the hip wave, whether there was a simple ratio, but he stopped himself from attempting to calculate the relative sizes from his visual recollection, although he believed he could, and that the ratio, in keeping with the theme of that distracting feminine obsession of his, might turn out to be one to eight. But no, thinking of feminine forms and shapes would not produce any innovative thoughts, only trap his mind in the most ancient, mind-simplifying, and numbing loop of desire. He should be above and beyond that.

Just then the bell rang. He went to the door, and there stood Miriam in a crimson dress and a white collar. Her lips looked fuller than before.

"I was so worried about you that…"

"I know your thoughts, I can read them," Tesla interrupted her.

"I'm not surprised. I believe you can read my thoughts and see right through me."

"It's much simpler than that; you've just written to me."

"You know, what happened between us was so wonderful and subtle and amazingly powerful I couldn't stop thinking about it. Can you kiss me? Just once? Long?"

"It would be dangerous. I might succumb to some disease that can't harm you, like an Indian exposed to European diseases."

"We could practice self-restraint. It wouldn't be that dangerous. Just one more time, can we? The excitement of your strange touch…"

"I didn't touch you."

"That's what I mean. You didn't but you did."

She sat on his sofa and pulled her skirt up a little so she could sit comfortably. The motion revealed the curve of the muscle behind her shin, the soleus muscle, and that too was a wave. The sofa was very close to the iron post that went into the foundation of the building. Suddenly Tesla had a thought that the physical waves from the oscillator, when increased in intensity, could excite her.

"Undress!" he said. He stood up and spread his arms and, with his pointed aquiline nose, he resembled a condor landing on a rock.

"What? I thought you didn't want to. And you can see through my clothes, I'm always naked to you."

"Maybe I can, but this is for you, so you can feel the cool air blowing away your heat aura. Undress, and you'll experience some fascinating rhythmic sensations."

"Is that a euphemism?"

"I don't do euphemisms."

She began to undress. It was an elaborate feminine undertaking. He remembered the saying, *It doesn't cost as much to undress a woman as it does to dress her.* The layers of velvet and silk went, and there she lay, naked, her shiny and ethereal white skin reflecting light, ghostlike, darkening the room, and Tesla stood, dizzy with admiration. He attached his electric oscillator and tapped the iron post gently. The iron rang with high-frequency after-sounds like a tuning fork.

"See what happens now. These simple mechanical waves, when added precisely, build up. Pretty soon, the building will shudder, and you will have a fine sensory experience."

The iron emitted deeper clanking noises as it received more and more taps. Gradually, metal objects around the loft began to resonate, and the table began to slide, in jerks, and as the floor was slightly tilted, it traveled toward the street window.

Miriam lay on the shaking sofa and lifted one of her knees above the other, and Tesla admired the angle of her thighs, estimating that if he averaged the lines, it would be thirty-two degrees, a very fine number indeed.

"What is going to happen next?" she asked.

"These resonating vibrations could grow to such an extent that in half an hour the buildings across the street would crack and tilt. If I kept it up for three hours, I could shatter all the buildings in New York."

"I don't believe you," Miriam said, her eyes twice their normal size.

"Yes, you believe me," he said, gazing into her eyes from beneath his drooping eyelids, calmly, as though refusing to mesmerize her. If he opened his eyes, he could send beams of electricity into her, but he didn't want that at the moment. On the other hand, if he let his eyelids droop too much, he saw her light, from his memory of her at the dinner table.

The floor shook and Tesla perceived slight vibrations through the rubber soles of his shoes. He preferred to wear expensive hand-crafted shoes to fit his long and narrow feet, but whenever he did experiments, even if they didn't directly involve electricity, he didn't want to be grounded, and rubber let him float in space as it were, electrically speaking. The shaking went into his bones and induced a prompt erection. He was surprised because he didn't think he was excited. He buttoned up his frock coat, certain she hadn't noticed the evidence of his lust. He wondered if it was lust for her or for the harmonic waves of the earth, and decided it was Miriam more than the waves of the earth, although the two did act in synergy at the moment, as did his oscillator waves.

It was cool in the apartment, and Tesla noticed goose bumps on her forearms and her buttocks.

"I love it, how you terrify me."

"I know that I could, if you gave me a few months, cause such violent vibrations in the crust of the earth that continents would split farther apart. New mountain ranges, higher than the Himalayas, would appear in Nebraska, and the Missouri would flow into the Hudson Bay."

"You're insane. Ah...keep on talking."

The floor shuddered. Two chairs hopped and squealed and circled around each other as though two drunken, invisible musicians couldn't contain their melodies to their instruments. The sofa shook and slid rhythmically, a few inches with each impulse. On the bookshelf, a bottle of golden-hued slivovitz danced, tilting minutely and progressing toward the edge.

A hue of red, of the blood in rhythmic motion, surfaced down her neck and breasts. Her breasts rippled in circular waves, which spread from the nipples outward; her breasts rippled like two puddles after swallowing tossed pebbles. Tesla gazed, adoring the responsiveness of her flesh.

"I can make an earthquake just for you, my dear."

"It's the first time ever you've called me 'dear.'"

"And as a matter of fact, I believe we already have an earthquake, and since we are in the epicenter of it, we're quaking the least." Tesla walked to the window. Several houses up the street, windows were bursting, people ran, old roof tiles slid and crashed on the pavement. Hm, maybe that's getting a little too far? Tesla thought, but he wanted to finish his point. "If you gave me a year or so, provided that I found out the exact harmonic formula for the Earth, I could split the Earth in half. It would split like a ripe watermelon when you stick a knife into it just an inch."

"Ah, ah!" Miriam turned pale. "Touch me, please!"

"We don't need to go that far, now, do we?" Tesla asked. "Of course, I would have the technical problem of keeping the oscillator so solidly fixed somewhere that all the shaking around it wouldn't dislodge it and bury it. You know, at a certain point, the oscillator would commit suicide before the mission was accomplished. Anyhow, if I found an iron vein, both firm and elastic enough, running down into the earth…"

"Suicide? Oh, would you like to die with me? I love the idea! We could attain ecstasy while simultaneously dying together."

At that moment the sofa slid halfway across the loft.

Windows across the street fell out all at once with a shattering burst.

"Ah, ah, don't stop!" Miriam gasped and grew as red as the velvet of her discarded dress.

"This is working even faster than I thought," said Tesla. He grabbed a sledgehammer and smashed his oscillator. The shaft of iron resounded so loudly that Tesla thought his eardrums must have burst.

Miriam leaped out of the sofa that had crashed against the wall. She gathered her robes and she slid on her silk stockings and other undergarments and held her dress, figuring which way would be the best to enter it, when the police barged in.

"Sir, the neighbourhood is falling apart. Is that you and your mad experiments?"

"No, gentlemen. I'm engaged in other gentlemanly activities, if you don't mind."

"Oh, I see," said one policeman. "Sorry to bother you."

"Not at all. I am glad you are around. I was becoming worried myself."

Miriam was trembling as she put the dress on.

"Come back next week, and we'll see whether my low-frequency radio waves combined with microwaves could excite you."

She smiled at him, her lips curving and intensifying in light.

"We can do better, next time. I can make fantastic microwaves, which a German now calls Röntgen rays, although I discovered them a while back. I forgot to file the patent for that one. Do come back, and I'll send beams through you, and you might like it. I could show the exact layout of your bones. Do you know the angle of your pelvis?"

She walked out, and he accompanied her. The building still seemed to shake with aftershock waves, which resonated in Tesla's bones, even in his pelvis. There was the debris of shattered glass, bricks, tiles along the walls.

As he walked in the streets, he didn't listen and he didn't talk. He was melancholy since he spent too much time thinking about raising money for his experiments, and now he wondered whether he would be able to shake off the thoughts of Miriam's curves and coils. He used to be able to come up with a patent every ten minutes during his walks, but at this rate maybe it would be one a day. His priestly father did warn him against money and women. Nikola should be able to forget her curves, or humanity would languish in darkness for a millennium to come.

When he said goodbye to Miriam absentmindedly, looking at shattered windows above her head rather than at her, she stood on tiptoe. Her lips embraced his lower lip. In surprise, he didn't withdraw right away, and her lips squeezed his softly and irresistibly, like some kind of submarine creature its meal. And as though an electrical eel had gripped his lip, a scorching sensation shot deep through him, and a freezing one enveloped his skin.

He stepped back, and the glass shards on the cobbles screeched and cracked beneath his feet. Her frizzy hair apparently pulsed blue light blindingly. He ran. Even when he reached his door-step, he felt the hot lips printing their vertical lines on his lip, and he shivered, thinking of the millions of invisible creatures crawling inside his lip onto his gums, tongue, throat, and lungs. He leaped up the dusty and dank stairs to burn his mouth with slivovitz. As he slammed the door behind him, the bottle tipped over the edge of the shelf and crashed on the floor, and the salvific spirits sank into the thirsty wood.

IN THE SAME BOAT

A white sailboat rattled through the waves of the Pacific with the North American continent as a rugged blue shade in the background, like a distant and violent oceanic storm. The thumping of the boards against the hissing waves mesmerized the two men in the boat. The sunshine permeated their skins and warmed their bones; they had surrendered themselves to the sun, the god of the Incas. Peter, blond and pink with his large, translucent blue eyes, blinked, and his pupils shrank to two points to protect against so much light. Francisco's narrowly set eyes flickered through long eyelashes above his thin, aquiline nose. They both wore white T-shirts that didn't hide the lines, curves, and teeth of their muscles.

On the second day of their journey, they woke up as the sun was buoying out of the ocean. Francisco sang *Gracias a la vida*, stretching his arms wide as if to embrace the sun; his armpit hairs sprouted out of his shirt, and thick blue veins calmly branched from his biceps over the elbow into his forearm. Peter rubbed his thick eyelids and ejected his night-spittle overboard.

On a propane cooker, they grilled fish they'd managed to catch in a salt-eaten net. They separated the flesh and the bones and threw the white comb-like skeletons with slanted ribs into the grape-colored water. The sun scattered its bronze radiance over the sky, and Francisco and Peter fell asleep, dreaming the second day and the second morning were good.

On the third day, they fished, ate, worshipped the sun without looking at it directly, just as Moses could not look at God's glory but only at the radiance that went after Him. The water sprinkled over their skins now and then, enough to soothe them against the sun. No border patrol was in sight. They felt the day had been good.

The fourth day the tranquility became boredom. They no longer paid attention to the sun and failed to worship it. They talked with their voices dry, recalling anecdotes from their recent past. They went over the details of their friendship the way lovers would.

They had met in Gillette, Wyoming, playing pool in a bar where laid-off oil rig hands hung around—some missing their fingers, and some who clenched beer cans in artificial fists of steel.

"What are we playing for?" Peter had asked.

Francisco replied: "For your Social Security number!"

"If you want my IRS problems and debts, go ahead!" Peter had dropped out of Baylor Medical School after his first year, with his student loans exceeding thirty thousand dollars. Without an SSN, Francisco, as an illegal alien from Mexico, could not hold a job for more than one paycheck period, fearing that the Immigration & Naturalization Service agents would track him down. So Francisco worked on Peter's SSN, on an oil rig as a worm, splitting his salary with Peter, and sometimes Peter worked and Francisco stayed back; they counted as one person for the social security administration. They stayed together in a bunkhouse, drank vodka, and shot pool every night, and nearly every dawn Francisco, badly hung over, put on his gloves and a cracked plastic helmet and pushed drilling pipes dangling from the derricks, one over another, until one struck him in the head and knocked him out with a brain concussion. He had refused to be taken to the hospital, scared that after his papers were scrutinized he would be tossed in jail or over the border. So he recovered with Peter in the bunkhouse, drinking Coke and reading a *National Geographic* report on the Incas. He fancied himself in Machu Picchu, in golden robes, glittering in the sun, surrounded by lovely bronze maidens, supple dancers coiling around him. Did they sacrifice the maidens? Did they eat them? He had talked about the Incas so much that Peter said, "You must've been an Inca king in one of your previous lives to have these vivid dreams first thing, as you recover from a concussion!"

Francisco suggested they should go to the Andes and live like poets on the beauty of the mountains. They were sober when they decided to go to Peru, and in genuine Peruvian manner they reconsidered their decision when they were drunk. Three days later, liking the decision in both states of mind, they adopted it. Peter dreamed of collecting ancient pottery and selling it to Sotheby's in London. They chose the cheapest form of transportation with the fewest number of borders: the wind and the ocean. They had stolen a sailboat named *Kon-Tiki* in Santa Monica, California.

Now, on the boat, they went through their stories many times and they told each other many anecdotes. Peter told this one: During the Great Depression in Berlin, it was not advisable for well-fed provincial girls to get off the train at the Friedrichstrasse station, looking for work, because they could reappear at the station as sausages sold to the hungry passengers. A butcher there would offer employment only to slaughter and then process them through sausage-making machines.

On the eighth day of their journey, they ran out of stories. The image of the high jungles and icecaps of the Andes paled in their minds. They fished, ate chunks of flesh from the ocean, and yawned.

On the twelfth day, the horizon kept tilting; frothing water spat out from the waves, which resembled broken teeth cracking once again while the new ones rose through the dark indigo gums. In the evening, a great wind plunged into the ocean and the ocean leaped into the wind to drive it away, but the wind only grew windier at that. Lightning flashed and the high, long waves carried the boat up and then laid it down low, as if on a railless rollercoaster. The waves screamed and howled and hissed like thousands of lions and snakes, but they did no harm to Peter and Francisco. By the morning, the tired storm lay down, thin, prostrate, and the ocean became as calm as a glacial lake. The sun, the bald Old Man of the Sky, reddened, as though ashamed of his violence, and the heat of his cheeks warmed the waters.

The friends lost count of days.

One day, perhaps the thirtieth, Peter cast the net into the water. For a long time no fish hit the net, and Peter yawned. All of a sudden something big smashed into the net. The ropes cracked and would have pulled Peter overboard but for Francisco grabbing his hand. A shark dragged the boat the way a horse drags a sled over the blue snow. Francisco fired his gun. Some red mixed with the salty foam, resembling a strawberry shake. The shark convulsed and pulled so vehemently that Peter and Francisco and the gun fell overboard. The men quickly swam to the boat, which floated away from them just as quickly. With the image of the shark jaws snapping their feet, they plunged their arms into the water, splashing. Francisco reached the boat and extended an oar to Peter, then lifted him aboard.

They gasped and when they grew hungry several hours later, they realized that they had lost their net, their food.

Peter had once fasted for three weeks, drinking a gallon of spring water a day, and when his mother saw him after it, she burst into tears. He smiled at the recollection.

They had to ration their water, which was down to three gallons.

They sliced the sail to make a net. They managed to catch nothing; another big fish tore the net.

Five days later they lay in a stupor, no longer hungry. Big ocean liners and tankers noiselessly passed by at a great distance, and Peter and Francisco at first stood up and hollered and, later, as they watched ships slide noiselessly over the line of the horizon like setting suns, they gave up.

Francisco missed the earth more than he missed women. When he got a morning erection, he masturbated, as if his sperm could promise life, and he imagined not luscious women but grassy ravines and rivers. Ejaculating, he watched his sperm fall onto the boards and ooze.

Peter shouted, "You idiot! What a waste of energy!"

"True, maybe a whole hour of my life."

"Maybe your whole life because you could be short of the shore that one hour. But what am I saying? We'll make it. We've got to believe it."

"Power of positive thinking, ha? I don't even know for sure what the coast looks like." Francisco kneeled and licked his sperm the way a cat laps milk.

Peter said, "That's some improvement. If you have to do it, at least eat it. But your body can never restore the energy you lose through the sperm. At best, the body can use only about thirty percent of the energy from food."

They both dozed off and neglected to steer the boat. Peter woke up and shouted at Francisco. Francisco seated himself and steered.

Peter was falling asleep again, falling a-dead. His body was stringy and dry and his blood moved slowly. His every breath, every motion, was slow; he felt his body was precise, with its sensation of bodily control stemming from its opposite, the lack of control. He admired his minimalistic body economy, pure, neatly abstract, a spirit with hallucinogenic visions: waterfalls, filled with the luminosity of the sun, splashing over him. He awoke with his throat parched and sore, and thought, I can have only two glasses of water a day. If Francisco weren't here, I could have four!

When Francisco fell asleep, Peter poured himself an extra glass of water, water stolen from Francisco's blood. Peter's hand trembled. His Adam's apple leaped like a stone in a rough brook as he gulped the water.

Francisco groaned in his sleep as if aware that his plasma was being drunk. He awoke and touched his face, eclipsed by bones. His eyes glowed, and he narrowed them because the platinum sunrise was too brilliant. He squinted at Peter; Peter's eyelids were nearly fully drawn over his eyes, their skin creased and purple.

They stared at each other with an acute, shared consciousness. What were they now? Still best friends? How could they be? Friendship is the highest form of being human, and they were no longer human nor animal; they were dying life, and dying life like a wounded lion knows no mercy, no friendship, only struggle and revenge. Neither could seek vengeance on his own self. They could not attack a shark, they could not attack the ocean, they could not attack the sky. They could attack only each other.

Peter appeared to Francisco stranger than any stranger, slowly disappearing from his sight and mind, and his sight and mind were slowly disappearing also.

Peter's heart thumped against his rib cage at the thought that Francisco was flesh. Meat. He could kill Francisco, eat him, and live. But how could he, his best friend? A raspy voice kept repeating in his ears, somewhere from within: "Kill him, kill him, killim, killim, killm, kill!" He shuddered, and thought that it would be better to kill him or be killed by him than that both of them die. He thought about the Incas with their human sacrifices. They would have the Andes right on the ocean; two hungry men with nothing to eat but their flesh. Flesh is singular. There are no porks, sheeps, fleshes; it's all one. Peter lustfully stared at Francisco's *musculus gracilis,* the graceful and lean muscle crossing the inner thigh.

Peter's blood cried like the spilled blood of Abel, except that Abel's blood shrieked against murder and Peter's for it.

Francisco let his arm hang loose overboard, staring into the water like a cat at an aquarium; his teeth chattered, and soon he dozed off. Peter wondered, Maybe he doesn't want to kill me. Maybe he doesn't know I want to kill him. How could he sleep otherwise?

Peter could not sleep. Even when snoring, he was half awake. Fearing death, he was exhausting himself and inviting it.

Presently, Francisco woke up and stretched his arms. Peter didn't look him in the face, thinking that the seed of murder that was growing in his blood must have reached his eyes, lurking in them. They each had a glass of water, their only glass for the day; their rations were down to one gallon.

Around noon, the sky and the water turned gray and dark. The air was musty with water hanging between sky and ocean. Yet the water wouldn't fall.

Francisco said, "It will rain."

"Why?"

"My leg hurts where I broke it years ago playing soccer. The leg knows."

The water suddenly fell from the air above them; it fell into the ocean in massive avalanches. Peter and Francisco opened their mouths like baby hawks awaiting their mother to drop torn sparrows into their beaks. They tried to collect the water in a fragment of the plastic boat cover.

The flashing and lightning through the darkness seemed like a dance of death to Francisco. He was homesick for the land. The real homeland was down there, buried in the grace of the ocean. When I'm dead, maybe none of my bones will be buried in the soil, not even on the ocean floor. Sharks will tear me apart. Maybe one of my molars will touch the floor, heavy with gold.

Francisco touched the golden tooth, a memento from the earth, from rocks—the purest part of a rock, used for dirtiest greed, dividing people into rich and poor. It comes from the ground but is not ground because the ground is never pure. Gold is a symbol of purified self because it has no traces of the soil or anything else; it is only itself—noble, and it inspires you to try to become noble, a pure self detached from everybody, selfish to the extreme, inhuman. A human being is a mixture of elements and cultures, and to strive to create anything purely individual, purely mono-cultural, is purely monstrous.

They collected several gallons of water.

After the storm, the sky cleared, the ocean pacified, and though Peter and Francisco had filled their stomachs with water, they were dizzy. Francisco looked at Peter's shoulder, several streaks of muscles, and felt like chewing them. He thought he was merely entertaining himself with the fantasy, but it took hold of him. Can I kill Peter? How? Maybe the oar could smash his skull. How can I think like this? Peter is my only friend. But we are animals; life is above everything. Life means eating life. Life communally survives on love, individually on hatred. Only mothers can die for their children, mothers and Jesus Christ. Haven't I always been a cannibal? As a child I sucked my mother's breasts, draining her flesh. I longed to taste the salt of her blood through the salt of milk, trying to replace the blood that used to come to me through the umbilical cord, to flow through me like alcohol through an alcoholic. Maybe only those of us who remember our mothers' blood become alcoholics, trying not to forget but to remember. We started with the mother; our basic nature stems not from the assassination of the father but from the slow killing of the mother.

Francisco was startled at his thoughts, as if it wasn't him thinking, but someone else in him. Harboring the thought that he should kill Peter or that Peter would kill him, Francisco could no longer sleep. Half awake, he tightened his hand on the oar. Without saying a word, each knew what the other was thinking, their alertness incriminating them.

Nights unsettled them. Francisco constantly imagined himself taking up the oar and crushing Peter's skull. It would take too much time. Peter would notice. They sat on the opposite ends of the boat. It was the third week of their starvation. They saw all the flickers of the light: is that a knife blade flickering? They heard all the rustling of waves: is he getting up to kill me?

A dawn at the end of the three weeks of starvation announced the divine splendour of the sun. The sun was scarlet. They both looked at it in amazement and then at each other's faces, overcast with a red hue; their eyes were bloodshot. They watched each other through a prism of blood, all the salty rainbows of the world collected in one color, rusty red.

They looked at each other with pity, too, regretting to see biology vanquish their spirits. Their spirits were still friends, right then in the calm, as they reconciled themselves with death and didn't care to listen to the voices within them. Tears appeared in their eyes, at the same time. They no longer cared for life at all costs. Peter was ashamed of his knife. But to throw it away would be to acknowledge that he had imagined a murder scenario. The scenario was hovering in the air, resembling a dome painted by Michelangelo: pink muscles of edible flesh, elongated, darkened, as if Peter's ceiling was filled with Franciscos stretching and flexing their flesh in various postures; Francisco's filled with many Peters, while some deltoid and trapezius muscles floated detached, like doves and kites. But to acknowledge it required too much courage.

Friendship somehow resurged. In their muscular chapel, they had both concluded that they were animals and not humans struggling to live. That was an exaggeration; thought usually is. Their friendship now spited their arteries. The salty tears, the bit of the oceanic water that rose through their eyes, were salty from blood yet not bloody.

Their eyes protruded out of deeply creased skin, piously gazing at the sharp outlines of their muscles. Their veins ran along like branches of a leafless tree.

A tooth irritated Francisco, and he shook it between his forefinger and thumb. The tooth remained in his fingers. Blood gushed and he spat it. Peter kneeled and licked the foamy blood off the boards. Francisco sucked his own gums.

Peter's gums bled too, and Peter swallowed the blood thirstily.

They continued to stare at each other with pity, love, and hunger. Their own blood shook them and crossed out their white flags of peace with death. The red shade disappeared from the sun but, through their drooping eyelids, the light still assumed an orange hue. In the evening the sun was larger and redder than they had ever seen it. The gory circle pushed toward the ocean slowly and unstoppably. It stabbed the ocean, cutting its stomach open; the true color of the ocean came out of the blue veins—red, echoing the sky and the sunken god of life and violence, the sun. The ocean swallowed the Old Man of the Sky without a sound.

The waves played with the bronze light as if lulling it to sleep. The light moved with each wave, evasive, unsubstantial, luring the eyes back to murder. The sky turned a gloomy indigo, as though it were a gigantic blood vessel. The full moon with its dried-up oceans slipped out, eclipsed. Its light cast down an unprocessed film that, once sunk in the chemicals of the ocean, began to develop; pictures appeared slowly, with emerging contrasts.

Their eyeballs flickered in the dark, like four candles at a medieval plague carnival.

I should have killed him as soon as I woke up, thought Peter.

I should grab the oar, thought Francisco.

No choice, thought Peter. I can't wait and wait. If I fall asleep again, he'll kill me.

Peter began to move slowly, holding an empty glass in his hand, as if he would fill it with water to drink, and in his other hand, behind his back, he gripped the ivory handle of his hunting knife. Francisco tightened his muscles. Why did Peter move so slowly if he wanted to drink? Peter moved slowly like a tiger that needs to hide its movements, but on the boat nothing could be hidden. Even the moon failed to eclipse. Francisco grabbed the oar, still heavy from the water, acknowledging the imminent struggle. Peter hesitated. Is Francisco strong enough to use the oar? I must act swiftly. What if he falls overboard and drowns? We'd both die.

Peter crept nearer. Francisco's muscles tensed more, and he jumped. The boat shook. He flew at Peter, swinging the oar. Peter ducked sideways. The oar missed his head and smashed his left shoulder, cracking the collarbone loudly. Peter fell on the boards, his knife flying out of his hand. The motion swayed Francisco and he fell over the bench. Peter was in a knockdown. He tried to stand up and collapsed again. Francisco lifted himself slowly and took up the oar. Peter's hand was reaching for the knife. Francisco was dizzy; the waves made it hard for him to keep his balance. Peter, the knife in his hand, his consciousness crimson, half stood and half leaped at Francisco, like a runner at the start of a race. Francisco started sideways. Peter missed and fell over Francisco's feet. Francisco kicked at his face but hesitated because he felt pity for the bleeding Peter. The moon was not eclipsed. It came out of a thick cloud, full.

Peter quickly stood up—the struggle actually fell together in slow, exhausted motions—and plunged and collapsed at Francisco again. Francisco jumped aside, but too slowly. The knife hit his rib cage, slid below it, and climbed into his liver. Peter pulled the knife out and stabbed again. Francisco lay against the rudder, blood spurting out of him to the rhythm of his heart. Peter stabbed again, aiming at the heart, and his knife got stuck in Francisco's rib, between the head of the rib and the sternum. Peter pulled it out and the bones crunched. Peter's shoulder was riven with scorching pangs of pain. He spat a couple of teeth from his mouth. Francisco stared at him with fervid fixedness.

Peter kneeled on his side and pressed his four fingertips (he didn't use the thumb) into Francisco's lukewarm skin on the neck for pulse; he pressed in the front of the transverse muscle running from the back of the skull to the collarbone and wasn't sure whose feeble pulse he felt, his or Francisco's. I should finish killing him. Peter lifted the knife in his hand and held it high. The blade smudged with blood flickered in the vague moonlight. He waited like Abraham when sacrificing Isaac, but no angels came from the sky to stop his hand, and there were no goats around the altar to be sacrificed in Isaac's stead. There was no faith to be proven; this was not a test. Out of pain in his shoulder more than resolve, Peter's hand came down. The knife slid between the collarbone and the upper ridge of the trapezoid muscle as smoothly as the sun had sunk into the ocean. Francisco's body convulsed, blood gushed; Francisco's frozen blue eyeballs crisscrossed, focusing somewhere behind Peter's neck. He opened his mouth, and to Peter it was not clear whether his throat gurgled in giving up his ghost or whether he said: rhrhood luckrh, the way a Dutchman might say Good luck. The light vanished out of Francisco's eyes.

Francisco's blood, no longer spurting in the rhythm of heart, flowed slowly and feebly. Peter licked the blood off the skin below the rib cage and sucked the wound behind the collarbone. And after that, numb, no longer in pursuit of blood, his warm awareness oozed below the surface of the ocean, through the limbs of octopuses, past orange and green fish glowing into the paradise beneath good and evil, spreading with ease throughout his body to his sore eyelids. Through his fluttering eyelashes, instead of one silvery moon, he saw four merging in and out of one. Silver light flashed at him from the lulling waves, never from the same place, never offering to be scrutinized. He leaned against the bench and the sideboards; his head was gently swayed in the rhythm of the ocean. The actorless play of elusive light went on for him.

The murmur and splashing of the waters was a purr of the oceanic mother cat suckling her kitten. The sounds changed and passed away, the light shifted, but the darkness always stayed in the ocean, steady and true. The warmth from within calmed his stomach, and the cool from the outside soothed his lungs and forehead, as if his mother's hand had touched him at the end of a long fever.

For breakfast, Peter cut through Francisco's left calf, amazed at the thickness of the skin. Shoes could be made of it. If a tent could be made of the foreskins of the Philistines David had killed, you could make shoes out of the skin; if you peeled off the skin of the foot and put it back together, you'd have a perfect foot-glove, a moccasin. Peter laughed, thinking how his thoughts displayed good Yankee ingenuity. He carved out the medial head of the *gastrocnemius*, cut the stubborn Achilles's tendon, and burnt the flesh on the propane cooker.

In the afternoon Peter grew bored. Now he had nobody to be tense with, nobody to keep him alert and conscious, so he dozed. But gradually, insomnia set in. And rather than turn away from the corpse, he turned to it, as if begging Francisco to talk to him. The body lay supine with the eyes closed, giving an impression of an iris-less sculpture, a Rodin bronze of a sleeping philosopher, the one Rodin would have made had he lived longer.

Peter wondered what he could do to kill the time. Why not study anatomy, the most basic of the humanistic as well as the natural sciences. He took up his knife, and with his thumbnail scratched the brown fragile sheets of blood from the blade. He began to peel the skin off the thinned left thigh. He tried to separate the layer of skin from the subcutaneous fat, but there was so little fat that it was no thicker than the *fascia lata* and the *perimysium*, the sheets enveloping the muscles below. Between the hardened thin layer of fat and the *fascia*, he freed the long saphenous vein, purple and limp. Then he cut sideways between *adductor longus* and *sartorius*, until he reached the femoral artery and vein, two-thirds of the way between the skin and the bone. He separated the muscles and reached for the femur. He cut lightly into the bone and peeled off the *periosteum*, the yellowish white sheet of bone. The femur was splendidly white, almost like the ivory handle of his knife. Throughout the *practicum* he was fascinated, highly alert and cautious, with his stomach growling. He tried to recall the objectivity of an anatomy lesson, the tightness of the corpse. His knife was much duller than a scalpel, and the fresh corpse was startlingly red compared with the old brown formaldehyde cadavers he had seen on TV. The procedure to him was like a scripted autopsy, as if the cause of death had to be determined. And what was the cause of death? Survival. Francisco had died from survival.

Peter began to separate the triceps and the biceps of the right arm, letting the muscle sheet stay with the biceps. He pressed the brachial artery, which bounced right back, and traced the artery as it arose through the muscles and ran closer to the bone *humerus*, gradually twisting from the medial side to the front of it. His finger got stuck against its branch, *profunda brachii*, coiling backward through the triceps. Next to the brachial artery, further from the bone, Peter separated a thick white string, *nervus medialis*, and though he pulled it as hard as he could, it wouldn't break nor slide much from between the muscles. Behind the string, close to the skin, ran a thinner string, the ulnar nerve, the funny-bone nerve that he remembered playing with as a kid, striking the edge of the breakfast table with the elbow, coffee cups, with violets clanking, sunny-sides-up trembling with little waves, his mother shouting, "Pete, for Heaven's sake!" while he concentrated on the electric tingle in his forearm. He had imagined swarms of ants covered his forearm, millions of little legs stepping inside his skin, skating over his muscles.

Peter stuck his knife into Francisco's crunchy sternum and tore through the abdomen to the navel, then to the pubic bone. He tried to pull the abdomen apart, but it was too tight, so he made a transverse cut through the navel, resulting in an inverse cross. He cut through several layers of muscles, each with fingers in a different direction, removed the abdominal wall with the peritoneum, the abdominal sheet, and plunged his hands into the slippery intestines. He stared at the many colors— pink, gray, brown, red, white—all impure, muted; there was a shade of blue in the ascending colon on the right, the transverse colon beneath the liver was still soaked in blood, the sigmoid colon on the low left was bluish. Upward, beneath the shrunken stomach, his fingers felt the tongue-like, spongy pancreas and the walls of the duodenum that enveloped the head of the pancreas, like a lover embracing his beloved. Peter, driven by curiosity to reach into the secrets of secreting matter, cut into the duodenum and found the opening of the pancreatic ducts in its wall, and cutting through the pancreas with his knife, he traced the common bile duct. He followed the pancreatic duct and felt the pancreas to the right as it thinned. He tried to pull it out, but it was firmly attached to the peritoneum in the back; he cut through the back peritoneum next to the bumpy spine and fingered the inferior *vena cava* and the rubbery *aorta abdominalis*. At the thin end of the pancreas, he touched the smooth surface of the kidney-like crimson spleen, squeezed it and cut it out, with blood dripping.

Peter tore out half a yard of the intestines and threw them overboard. Shouldn't I have used the intestines for sausages?

It was getting dark, and Peter interrupted his anatomy lesson; for supper, he simmered the spleen on the propane cooker.

Next pink dawn he recoiled from his sleep; he had been resting his head on a piece of Francisco's abdominal wall, torn and thin. What to do with the body, after the anatomy lesson? To embalm or not to embalm? He remembered what he had read about how the Egyptians did it. They stuck a hook through the nostrils into the brain and scratched inside the skull so the brain could flow out, and what remained of it was dissolved in natrum. They opened the inside of the body, took out the organs, and oiled the inner walls and sewed them back. And there was another method: you don't remove the intestines; you inject cedar oil into them through the anus, and the body pickles in natrum. After seventy days, the flesh it gone, and the skin remains taut on the bones, ready to last for thousands of years. But this was all useless to Peter; he had no natrum and he needed the flesh to eat.

To preserve the flesh as long as possible, he cleaned out the bacteria-rich intestines completely, because from them the rotting would spread. And then he paused, gazing at Francisco's corpse—well, it no longer belonged to Francisco, but to Peter; so, in a sense, he looked at his corpse.

He lifted some seawater in the bit of plastic boat cover; he soaked his clothes in the water. With the salt that remained after the water evaporated, he rubbed a whole assortment of muscles neatly filed on the boards: the broad *trapezius*, the broader *latissimus dorsi*, the twisting streaks of *pectoralis* with the swollen *deltoideus* above, *flexor carpi ulnaris sinister, rectus abdominis*, the tongue, and the heart, which, with severed blood vessels sticking out of it, lay like a defeated octopus. He sliced the heart, admiring how thick the wall of the left ventricle was.

He cut out the right lung, light and airy, wetly smooth, with little veins crisscrossing the surface, and he remembered what Francisco had told him—the Incas used to tell fortunes by tracing the vein patterns in the lungs of sacrificial llamas.

In the evening Peter gorged, anxious that there might not be enough food for him, and afterward he fell asleep.

A bell is tolling. The sun has not risen yet. Maybe it won't. The horizon is rosy, the streets brown, the sky azure. Many people in black walk along the cobblestones of a narrow streets. The sound of the bell blows cold air into the people's hearts, through the pores of their skins, drawing blood from their faces, ashen green under blue-black hairs. Peter walks toward the gathering. Two black horses, steam rising from their backs, pull a black hearse covered in stiff green garlands, with purple ribbons and golden letters. Four men carry an orange casket out of a gray bullet-riddled house. The bells cease to toll and only a buzzing echo remains, rising in pitch. All of a sudden, one of the four coffin carriers slips on a soft lump of green horse dung and the casket falls after him, crashes on his foot and cracks open on the cobblestones. From a white sheet rolls out a corpse, stiff and naked. Good chunks of flesh are missing. The bone of one leg is bare, as are the bones of one arm, white, without a trace of flesh. One half of the face is missing, with the hollow of a missing eye staring out from some spookily calm darkness. The screams of the crowd echo against the church as the corpse rolls downhill toward Peter. Peter recoils: the corpse at his feet is his, him.

He woke up, catching his scream as it was vanishing in the murmur of the ocean.

Six days after he had killed Francisco, Peter noticed a coast, a blue, rugged haze. Seeing patches of green in the gray haze, he was reassured. He threw Francisco's bones overboard. Some bones floated, others sank. Peter pushed the skull into the water, but it emerged, grinning with its fleshless mouth.

In the afternoon, Peter saw white high-rise hotels and a sandy beach covered with bronze and pink bodies, orange and blue parasols, yellow and red water floats. Soon his sailboat cut into the sandy gravel, screeching. Bathers ran aside from the path of the boat. They saw Peter's apparition: hollow cheeks, hollow orbits of the eyes out of which two sad and brutal eyes glowed, long salty blond hair, burnt brown skin, ribs showing through a salt-eaten shirt. He looked like a holy man or a forlorn lunatic or an adventurer who has survived a trip into the heart of a volcano. Popsicle-sucking children shrieked and ran away, lotioned men and women shrank back.

Peter walked straight to an outdoor café with the little white tables and small palms with red flowers and ordered *una cerveza*. That much Spanish he knew. A young olive-skinned waiter, his hairs greasily wet, combed in parallels, gave the beer to Peter, scrutinizing him through his long eyelashes. To Peter there was something familiar in the face. Peter paid, handing out one salty dollar, and asked: "Hotel?"

"*Esto completo*," answered the boy. He drew a map on the back of a page from a notepad, which said Oasis, directing Peter to the outskirts of the town. There, Peter found a small hotel on a slanted cobbled street. He rented a room and slept for a day straight. Next afternoon he went to a barber's to have his hair cut and his beard shaved. As the barber razed through the foam, tickling his neck with the gentle touch of the blade, Peter was uncomfortable; it would be so easy for the blade to cut beneath the muscle into the artery. Unlike Cain, Peter had no sign on his forehead to brand him as a murderer, yet he felt as though one was there. His sign, unlike Cain's, wouldn't protect him. But the shaving went on peacefully; the older barber, his eyes half-closed, whistled *Gracias a la vida*; the fresh smell of pines floated through the room, blaming and invigorating Peter, who kept his eyes closed. When the barber asked him to take a look, Peter was startled at seeing himself in the mirror. His face was much darker than it used to be. His eyes were smaller; they no longer had an optimistic and frank air about them.

Strolling in the streets, he was surprised at how much Spanish he understood; he had never studied it. He had many déjà vu sensations. After two or three days, he understood the conversations fully. Whenever he shopped, his English consonants were softened; he attributed that to his three missing teeth, which made him lisp and activate his tongue more, to roll his r's. His body felt different from what he was used to. His movements were faster, his eyes shiftier. He looked in the mirror. His eyes were no longer blue, but greenish, tending towards hazel. His nose was thinner and a bit aquiline. It seemed to him that Francisco stared back at him. Francisco's liquid glare cooled him. No, I must be hallucinating. I'm going out of my mind! Next morning, as soon as he woke up, he rushed to the mirror to convince himself that he had hallucinated the day before. Out of the mirror leered a dark-eyed face.

Although he used to despise religion, Peter walked into the bullet-riddled church across the square from his inn and listened to a sermon amidst incense. On both sides stood pale Jesuses with thick red rivulets flowing from their thorn-pierced foreheads, and even thicker rivulets out of the holes in the ribs. He recalled the crunching sound of his knife in Francisco's ribs, and shuddered at the monotonous words of the priest: *Porque el que quisiere salvar su vida, la perdera; y el que perdiere su vida por causa de mi, la salvara.* (For he who wants to save his life will lose it, and he who loses his life for my sake, will gain it.) Peter walked out of the cold church. The sun smarted his eyes. The bells began to toll, smarting his ears. His whole body was tense and sore.

Several days later he was on a steel Greyhound. As the bus neared the U.S. border, there was a dark low cloud in the sky. At the border, Peter handed his salt-eaten passport to a border policeman. A heavy-set border guard said, "Damn weather, it makes my bones ache!" Then he lifted his grey eyes and said, "But this isn't you! You're not Peter Cunningham."

"Yes, of course I am. What are you talking about?" said Peter.

Several border officials interrogated Peter. He asked to be allowed to call his mother in Cleveland, but when he came to dial, he couldn't recall her number. He had to call information, and only then did he get his mother's number. His mother's voice said, "You've got the wrong number."

"Bot, Modher, dhis is Pete…" A dial tone cut in.

He dialed again. Same thing. He dialed again. His father's voice shouted: "Can't you dumb Puerto Ricans dial right? Can't you at least read numbers?"

A cop said, "Enough of this circus. We could jail you or fine you, but since our jails are too full and you're a poor bum, we'll just let you go." The cop winked at him leniently. "You better steal a passport with a Hispanic name, or forge better. This one's on our records and so is your picture, so if you try again…" The officer spoke slowly as if Peter was too estupido to understand English.

A week later Peter entered the States in the hay of a truck along with three Mexicans. In Texas he looked for work in tomato fields. He began dreaming of going into the oil fields in Wyoming. He was confused, wondering what had gone wrong, and wished to start his self-analysis from his childhood, but though he had prided himself on vivid childhood memories, he could recall nothing concrete of Cleveland. Instead of images of suburban hedges with tricycles, aluminum trash cans, ovoid football, his mind produced images of llamas and women in black skirts under which children's heads lurk, little fingers picking noses.

After four weeks of work, on a day off Peter drove with several Mexicans in a mufflerless pickup to Benville. They bought beer at a 7-Eleven, and as they were about to enter their beat-up pickup, two police cars pulled up, flooding them with strong beams of light. Peter...but it would be better to call him Francisco from here on. Here we'll make a full stop because what would follow *sería una repetición de lo que había occurido tiempo ha; la entrada illegal de Francisco en los Estados Unidos, explotación en el trabajo, terror de la migra y...*

ACKNOWLEDGMENTS

These stories appeared, sometimes in different form, in the following publications:

"White Moustache"—*Tin House*
"Wino"—*Narrative Magazine*
"Dutch Treat"—*Witness*
"Be Patient"—*Narrative Magazine*
"Rasputin's Awakening"—*St. Petersburg Review*
"Crossbar"—*Zagreb Noir Anthology* (Akashic Press), and, in a longer form, *Guernica*
"Acorns"—*Narrative Magazine*
"When the Saints Come"—*Bridge 8*
"Heritage of Smoke"—*Exile Quarterly Review* (Toronto)
"Eclipse Near Golgotha"—*Barcelona Review*
"Wanderer"—*Narrative Magazine*
"Ideal Goalie"—*Barcelona Review*
"Strings"—*Literal Latte* and *Exile Quarterly Review*
"Remote Love"—*Blackbird*
"In the Same Boat"—*New Directions Anthology* #55

Many of the stories also appeared in a limited Canadian edition entitled *Ex-YU*, Esplanade Books/Vehicule Press.

I am grateful to the editors of the journals and anthologies for reprint rights, and to Guy Intoci, Dimitri Nassralah, and Michelle Dotter for additional editing on the stories in this book, as well as to John Goldbach, Tim O'Brien, Jeanette Novakovich, Bukem Reitmeyer, Jeff Parker, and Sasa Drach for reading some of the stories in progress.

I would also like to thank the Canada Arts Council, Yaddo, the Hermitage Artist Retreat, and National Endowment for the Arts for the time to write the stories.

ABOUT THE AUTHOR

Josip Novakovich is a Croatian-American writer who resides in Canada. His work has been translated into Croatian, Bulgarian, Indonesian, Russian, Japanese, Italian, and French, among other languages. He was a finalist for the Man Booker International Prize in 2013 and also received the American Book Award from the Before Columbus Foundation, the Whiting Writer's Award, and a John Simon Guggenheim Memorial Foundation Fellowship for Fiction, as well as a fellowship from the National Endowment for the Arts. His work has appeared in *The Paris Review, Threepenny, Ploughshares*, and many other journals, and has been anthologized in *Best American Poetry, The Pushcart Prize*, and *O. Henry Prize Stories*. He teaches English at Concordia University in Montreal, Canada.